(Novel)

Rami Siva Sankara Sarma

GEORGE

Grahaantaravaasi

(Telugu Novel)

by

Rani Sivasankara Sarma

Transformed into English by
an Alchemy All Its Own.

as

Vagrant's Tale

Mediated by

G.K. Subbarayudu

Ancient Stories have no Known Origins.
And No Predictable Endings.

Worldwide Circulation through Authorspress Global Network
First Published 2014
by
Authorspress

Editorial
Q-2A Hauz Khas Enclave
New Delhi-110 016

Marketing
E-35/103, Jawahar Park
Laxmi Nagar, Delhi-110 092

e-mails: authorspress@rediffmail.com; authorspress@hotmail.com
Website: www.authorspressbooks.com

Grahaantaravaasi (Novel)
ISBN 978-81-7273-734-4

Adapted from Telugu
by G.K. Subbarayudu

Printed in India at Tarun Offset, Delhi.

...more dimensionless than the point....
more areal than the surface

(An Aria of Ecstasy, Kuppa Srinivasa Sastry)

The shore exists shorelessly;
the water does not feel itself wet or cold...

("View with a Grain of Sand", Wislawa Szymborska)

Note on Spelling

In English, through only five (5) letters signifying vowels, it is possible to percieve and pronounce all short or long vowels and 'glides' contextually. Indian languages are quite different in this regard; they are explicit about the *Deergha* (long) and the *Hraswa* (short) vowels.

When diacritical marks are not used , Indian words need a different approach to spelling in English. I have consistently used two (2) letters for long vowels where I found it necessary:

Kanchinaadham

Bhoogola

Deepaavali

Gaayathri

Amaavaasya

Pishaacha

Deekshitulu gaaru

Daanavaaipera

Mukkaamala

udaasiino mahaabalaha

In one case, I spelt the word 'dark' as 'da..aa..rk'.

I hope readers will find this convenient; and hear Indian sound patterns instead of English *stress.*

G. K. Subbarayudu

Upfront

Kanchinaadham is my long-time friend. If he had any friends he could possibly speak of, I am one amongst them.

He died three years ago in a road accident in Chennapatnam. Why Kanchinaadham, who rarely left home, went that far afield is not known.

Recently I visited his home in Mukkaamala. The first house to the left of the banyan-tree turning, close to Mukkaamala Touring Talkies ... that's his. That house is largely in ruin. Datura plants grew in proud occupation of the walls. Sometime soon, even this remnant of memory will slip away from sight.

Why did I go there?

I have known since childhood that unsatisfied souls tarry about around unlit, ruinous houses. That's why I went there, perhaps. But no trace of Kanchinaadham was there.

Sitting on the promontory of this ruin-house I expressed my resolve to write as a book, Kanchinaadham's life-story. What's there to write? Kanchinaadham had said drily, without enthusiasm. The subject did not come up between us again. He has no regard for creativity. No faith in novel, inventive, probing expressiveness. Nothing new ever occurs; only the old recurs. The wheel keeps turning, that's it. The expanding universe shrinks and collapses into itself.

That‘s not all. Everything transforms into its other, dissolves into its contrary, Kanchinaadham said. This is Chairman Mao's sentence. Listening to Kanchinaadham reiterating it was like seeing all of contemporary history unfolding in ones mind. Everything completely turns into its contradiction. That's it. Whether Mao said it, or Kanchinaadham, this alone is Truth.

Part I

When I returned
from
the globe-moon,
the Earth had already
turned into
an alien planet

– Neil Armstrong

1

Terra Terribula... Bhoogola is boring ....Globe is galling... muttered Kanchinaadham. Slouching on the banks of the Mukkaamala canal, aimlessly flinging pebbles, he created this phrase for himself. He is suffering from the problem of lack of expression. Man's nature probably forms itself while still in its embryonic form in the womb. When exactly Kanchinaadham formulated the utterance, *Bhoogola is boring,* is not easy to tell. That he meditated upon the utterance millions of times in his solitude, is, of course, undeniably true.

When Kanchinaadham wished to speak about anything, he leapt into its exact opposite. This irrelevancy is probably traceable to his childhood, if not his very infancy.

Kanchinaadham's mother, Subbamma gaaru, used to tell the neighbours – our son began walking in circles round his dead grandfather's body. Thus circling, he went on saying, till they reached the funeral grounds – grandfather is sleeping. He is sleeping without snoring as usual. The boy just did not listen to any explanations that the grandfather was dead and had gone away to his Maker.

It was not just sleep and death – Kanchinaadham could not grasp the difference between most other things, either. During childhood, one Deepaavali day, he lit sparklers and let the florets fall on his hands. They singed sharply but did not burn. He did this many times... like in a game. Now he lit a flare, and let the large sparks fall in his palm. It burnt... one searing, painful burn. He bellowed and sobbed. Subbamma gaaru cursed – what the hell! How did you burn yourself! "Thought this won't hurt like the sparkler didn't," he wept.

Subbamma gaaru always kept saying, will you be able to remember your wife when married, or will you go away forgetting her in the bazaar?

Kanchinaadham did not face this problem.

Because he remained unmarried.

But he sunk deeper into the problem of inexpression. Mistaking one thing for another, inability to recognize, inability to create a clear and consistent utterance, was his permanent problem

He never undersood the meanings of his own utterances. But those utterances shadowed and haunted him, vexed him, insinuated into his sleep and forced him into wakefulness.

Bhoogola is boring is one such utterance.

2

Kanchinaadham's home is a call away from the Mukkamala Touring Talkies. Kanchinaadham's father Saambayya Deekshitulu's evening prayers were always swallowed by the cinema songs. Shut the windows... he bellowed ritually. *Om Bhoor bhuvas suvaha, shut those windows dammit...* this stayed permanently with Kanchinaadham, ... forever... though his father had died long since.

Yes, unrelated utterances got mixed up in his mind, always.

Once, Kanchinaadham visited his relations. It was Daanavaaipeta in the town Rajahmundry; connected portions of housing. He visited the common bathroom, and returned to his portion of the house. When he ambled into the bedroom, reality dawned suddenly. It was the adjacent portion! The couple on the couch were startled into untwining. Then again, it wasn't the husband but a lover!

Kanchinaadham beat a hasty retreat.

Objects, visuals, words – disability to recognize their distinctive features, was the permanent problem that Kanchinaadham faced.

On this basis, it was easy to account him mad, crazed or maladjusted. But, how to account for him is our problem. Not his. And this is how he lived out his first forty years.

Be it known that Kanchinaadham was his house name. But, surprise... surprise... that was his real name, too. Before he was born, two siblings had died, soon after the rituals of naming had been done. So Saambayya Deekshitulu refused to perform the naming ceremony this time. Thus grew Kanchinaadham, namelessly; and both surname and proper name settled on Kanchinaadham. In the school register his name was recorded as Kanchinaadham Kanchinaadham. Some teachers chose to cut it short to KK.

An abbreviated Kanchinaadham, KK, transited from the statement *Bhoogola is boring* into a more non-sequential expression of state. The expression was – '*Om Bhoor bhuvas suvaha* shut those windows dammit'. This sentence was his sole inheritance from father.

It was lunar eclipse. At the banks of Mukkaamala canal Lochs, Kanchinaadham stood neck-deep in water along with his father, Deekshitulu gaaru; father Deekshitulu gaaru commanded him to chant prayers till the end of the eclipse. Kanchinaadham went on chanting the *Gaayathri mantra.* Then woke up the KK in him. The lesson taught at school surfaced to memory. After the release of the eclipse, walking back home, he nudged father. American fellow set foot on moon and planted flag, they say? *Chandraloka* is a divine state; no one can go there, asserted Deekshitulu.

But the lesson on journey to the moon set KK floating in his dreams. Now one could take wing, fly away from the earth. Hope … that one could fly away from the galling globe entrapped between a changelessly dreary dawn and dusk; the intense hope and desire to launch out of the gravitational sphere of the earth … is ancient as Man.

Probably another world is quite similar? Man habitually keeps hope pined in unfamiliar, far off, unknown places (suffers blasts of devastation, too). But this hope is what keeps him walking in quest.

Kanchinaadham's schooling remained incomplete. It was his nature to leave all things part undone, in stages of incompletion. Even utterances; – when he spoke, a new sentence shoved itself into the previous sentence. He was the type...what type?... prototype of... one who barged into one portion of the house instead of another, and stumbled on to a sacred secret. Such was Kanchinaadham, alias KK, *aka* spoilsport.

Another instance from his childhood, another forbidden fruit. One Shuudra boy told him about two intertwined snakes rolling about. Though the mother tried to prevent him, saying it was evil, Kanchinaadham went and saw. He also pelted them with stones. They promptly slithered into the bush.

They were Cobras, snakes of time. They nurse revenge. Lifelong revenge. Follow wherever one goes. They are divines come from the netherworld of snakes. They have mystical powers. You ruined their romance, interrupted coitus. That's terrible offence against the divine. By the next new-moon night, *amaavaasya*, they will finish you – said one tribal lord, a fortune-teller, looming over him, terrifying him no end. Kanchinaadham was suitably horror-struck...all of ten years that he was.

The tribal accompanied Kanchinaadham, and apprised Subbamma gaaru of the impending disaster. She promptly fell into a breast-beating, wailing routine, common to helpless women. What your boy has done is great wrong; but I have a *mantra,* an antidote, the kind-cool looks and grace of the Hill-Goddess, said the holy hill-tribal. He left with a huge measure of rice, turmeric and *kum-kum,* and plenty of vegetables in return for intervention between Kanchinaadham and the crack of doom.

Kanchinaadham went to Rajahmundry for the purpose of education. Meetings of Rationalists went on aplenty, there. One speaker said that vengeance of snakes was a superstition. But to Kanchinaadham, the feeling persisted that some unseen presence always followed him. As if an invisible cobra waited upon him with vengeance in mind, always gobbling up his inner spirit and excitement. From the very beginning.

God!

Did tradition suck her down the canal drains of convention? Did vicious cobras of time swallow up sister's life?

They are terrifying, lurking silently in the deep dark dungeons of *paataala.* That cavernous depth swallows up all light. Turns thousand solar systems into light trivialities. From childhood, he had heard numerous stories after stories about *paataalaas,* dark caverns and the great sinuses that connected the earth to the depthless dungeons. *Akkayya,* elder sister, also narrated such stories. All those became a part of his language, integral to his utterances, to his very grammar. Seeing the sad face of his sister in solitude – he felt the flaming furnace of his language forged, and float sentences such as, 'she is falling without end; she is being stung by the dark serpent of time'.

Kanchinaadham, turned KK, read some books on geo-science and astronomy. Space science unveiled the blackhole to him. The blackhole gulps down light, too. Disdains the speed of light.

Said Saambayya Deekshitulu "dead or alive, she's no matter to me." Actually, what did that sentence mean? Is akkayya alive somewhere, and dead somewhere else, cancelling her materiality?

Averred Deekshitulu – "It's not in our family-nature, our homely character; never even knew a shuudra neighbourhood. And she eloped with a shuudra!" Subbamma stopped him short – "*Ayyooo,* that's not true…!"

Brahmin girl's corpse surfaced in Palivela Lochs, it appears! And Subbamma began wailing. Her howling did not stop, ever…

Demonic – dusk. Deekshitulu did not commence his ritual evening prayers. Such violation of traditional practice, he had never known before. Kanchinaadham walked on to the bridge. Flowing sounds of the canal resonated. Sounded like a funeral band. Didn't that canal carry in its flow the stories of several deaths?

Many years ago an infant corpse floated in this canal; swollen larger than infancy. Kanchinaadham saw it. He was only twelve then. Onlookers watched curiously, the body awash on the bank. Many, many onlookers. The TV hadn't yet come...The whole town flocked for every little event.

Kanchinaadham scurried home. Amma, corpse in canal, he said fearfully; child's corpse in canal.

Subbamma clamped her hand on his mouth. "Don't talk", she said. "Forget this", she said. She was trembling with fear, and anxiety.

Midnight, he was startled awake. "Amma! It's frightening… the child's corpse…"; "quiet, Quiet!" hissed Subamma.

"What? What's he saying" – asked Deekshitulu.

"Nothing, just a nightmare… bad dream," said Subbamma.

"Nooo ammaa, really…"

Subbamma clamped his mouth shut. "Lie down, sleep. What are fears to one who chants the Gaayathri mantra? Don't recall unnecessary things," Subbamma said.

Through the window, darkness spread into every crevice of the universe. Being accustomed to ritual obeisance thrice a day, he was keenly aware of the *tithi*: it was *amaavaasya*, new moon, da..a..ark night.

Kanchinaadham could not sleep.

Why was mother avoiding mention of that corpse? Whose child was it? Where did it drift from? Kanchinaadham's head fumed with fret. Gradually he drooped into a haze. As he drifted in sleep, the infant's corpse whirled in the whorls of water. Bobbed up and down, back and forth in the waves.

He was now in wake. That night brought no more sleep, nor any reference to the corpse either. He observed his mother weeping, face tucked into her bedsheet. Could not probe why mother was weeping.

That midnight, why mother wept, why the unknown infant's corpse troubled her so much, who the biological mother was – were questions that bothered Kanchinaadham no end. These secret queries left a deep chasm wide, between Kanchinaadham and mother. Whenever he spoke with her, the disruptive child-corpse came haunting back and cut the utterances short. The conversations thus remained abrupt.

Who can tell! This chasm between mother and child could have led to the insoluble problem of his ruptured, tortured language.

Kanchinaadham appears as if conversing in some code from a distance beyond this planet. Ask him what his name is! Kanchinaadham cannot reply immediately… even today. After a few moments elapsed he'd stutter.. umm..mm my name is Kanchinaadham. What do you do? Eh... what do? I do… doo…

Nothing. This is how his utterances stretch, and snap, as if some powerful ghost is holding them back. He looks as if he is not yet accustomed to this earth.

Devadas is the cinema Kanchinaadham saw most number of times. First he saw the cinema from half – way through. That, too, at the Touring Talkies of Mukkaamala. At that talkies, only ten year – old cinemas played. If you wanted to see today's cinema, you'd have to wait ten years.

Just as we must wait ten or twenty light-years to view far away stars, viewing the present at the Mukkaamala Touring Talkies entailed the lapse of lo…o..ong time.

However, before the movie ended, whenever one went, as many as went, a ticket could be had. If you appeared a slightly educated person, in a trouser and shirt, they'd dust some rusty old chair and invite you to sit. Mukkamala Touring Talkies was one *pushpaka*, an infinitely accommodative airbus.

Now… watching cinema at this talkies was a strange, exciting experience. As if one were watching the first cinema made after the invention of the first camera. Sometimes the picture became unclear, blurred. At other times it turned into a silent movie. The reel would snap. The cinema travelled back and forth. Events and times lost track of each other, became asynchronous. Cinema's evolutionary dynamics flashed on the screen… suffering this terrible torture with the purpose of improving future cinematic technology, no doubt.

At that talkies, every movie felt like the comatose, delirious state between Stage and Cinema. The cry 'once more' made them repeat the song. A scene that went by came back like a haunting roundelay. A three-hour cinema played for five to six hours.

Kanchinaadham's eternal favourite play was *Harishchandra*. Shivasri, an actor, played the role of Harishchandra numerous times on the *Dasara Navaraathris* at Amalapuram, Kotthapeta. When he sang "as destiny assigned, so duly suffered,"[1] it was clear that man could not escape the play of destiny. As he voiced, "King become commoner, attender turn emperor, in tune with the diktat of eternal time,"[2] it felt as if every man was but a twig in the torrent of time. Such a great emperor having to sell his dearest wife and child, transformed into a burial-guard, bound to undischargeable debts, rupturing riveted relations...

Similarly Devadas, son of a Zamindaar... Was society so comprehensively powerful? Does society exist today, too? That was the story before independence. Is the situation the same today? Is there a clash between past and present, now, too? Or have times changed? Stars are visible through the rust-eaten ceiling of Mukkamala Touring Talkies. Mosquitoes biting audience inside must be driven away only by the in-rushing winds from outside. Very modern, advanced theatres have now come to exist. Mukkamala Talkies, however, continues to stand. Perhaps there are some superficial renovations. But the tin-shed continues to be the roof overhead. Even now, years-old cinemas continue to play in a time-warp.

Kanchinaadham recalled the song, "Know this is dream nor/ know this is real/know this is life/yes, know this is life."[3] The reel had snapped two or three times and the song repeated, burying itself deep in his mind. For us, actually, cinema had not begun. Old-time verse drama had now changed its name to cinema. Saying KK was the same thing as saying Kanchinaadham. Drama and cinema were the same. Camera's wizardry hadn't begun. The magical wizardry of camera that could bring all secrets into the open, display the visual world in the glory of real flashing light, had not yet begun. Modern realism hadn't begun. "World is illusion, life is illusion, this, O man, is the simple essence of the Vedas."[4] Who could undo this illusion? Who could compose the grief of Devadas, the grief of Harishchandra? The secret weeping over the orphan child's corpse, that midnight … who could bring to life the grief of that anguished cry? That is *kaarmic* relationship; old debts can never be settled; the past always continues to shadow. The present continues to blaze in the entrails. Mukkamala Touring Talkies will never have a new movie. Some ancient grief, ancient memory, some ancient moan, weary, worn out, will resound there. Always.

Now, Kanchinaadham, standing on the Mukkamala bridge, eyes riveted in the depths of waters, was all of forty five years. He was only ten when he watched Devadas at the Mukkaamala Talkies. Has time changed between then and now? Has society changed? Did new water flow under the bridge? Really, is new water necessary? Does that cleanse ancient evil? Or does it bear new pollutions? It's not as if there is no change. Once, boats with open sails raised, floated slowly along, ever so silently. Wood-rafts helped pedestrians across to the other bank. Launches ran, raising waves in their wake. Not anymore. Wherever eyes went, bridges sprang. Motor vehicles wheeled. All this signalled technological change that came over the last decade.

Many other changes flooded Konaseema. In many locations, shrimp-farms swallowed thousands of acres of paddy fields. Devastating cyclones ravaged coconut groves. Landlords who hardly stirred enough to digest their glass of buttermilk, also realized the futility of trust in land. Should go to cities, or fly off to foreign lands in pushpakas, airbuses. Only the unusable stayed in Konaseema. Especially, the younger generation Brahmins experienced this change.

"Did Konaseema remnants exist?" asked Kanchinaadham. He peered keenly in all directions, like an Intergalactic-Being peeping into the life of an unknown planet. Was it the Konaseema he had known? Konaseema... what a beautiful name! How beautiful a place! But in its entrails flowed grief; the grief of orphaned infants flowed, Brahmin women's secret silent grief flowed.

Admitting a patient in Shravani Hospital in Amalapuram, said Sundaram uncle, was like entrusting the person to death.

Subbamma was on her deathbed.

At Shravani Hospital.

At that very juncture of time, Kanchinaadham met Sarma in a bar at Amalpuram. Sarma was a priest in a temple in Kothapeta. That temple had been built recently. Sarma was a fierce advocate of poetry. Had committed to memory, every verse from Sri Sri to Tripuraneni Srinivas. At every opportunity, he would cite some verse. Sarma had acquired a degree, but it was discontinuous, like rain-interrupted schooling in small towns. Took to priesthood for filling the stomach. Occasionally crawled into bars with friends. And savoured libations for the soul, looking hither and thither, observant, lest someone should observe him. His was a double-life.

Sarma said to Kanchinaadham, "Look man ... medicine has become merchandise. Doctors here pooled up to establish a centre for CT scanning. Spent lakhs for that; so, advised tests... necessary or not. Madden with medical tests. Squeeze money. Trouble transit–halters with unnecessary tests, instead of letting them go peacefully to meet their Maker. Make them speed and post unduly. It is difficult to ascertain which test is necessary, which not. After all the testing, they diagnosed nothing."

Sarma lit a cigarette; recalled a poem titled 'Dying – Differently' Men of different kinds, bodies of diverse classes, diseases of divergent strains; can machines make sense out this infinite set of differentia? Conversation between men is getting to be impossible, very complex. Then what can man achieve through the language of machines? Mantra's place has been usurped by machines. We believe doctors great in proportion to the dazzle of their machines. We feel satisfied that good health-care has been given, in proportion to the number of tests carried out, the number of machines to whose mysterious codes we have submitted our bodies. And now, said Sarma, there is no other go.

Kanchinaadham veered strongly towards the view that Subbamma's end was near. Doctor carried out different tests and finally diagnosed that it was a heart ailment. As much was diagnosed by the Mukkaamala quack earlier, by the grand device of a pulse-check. Kanchinaadham felt remorseful that he was putting mother through the torture of unnecessary tests at this terminal stage. Hippocrates had advised that in certain situations death not be averted. Necessary, natural, healthy death should not be prevented. This is part of the Hippocratic Oath that doctors ritually take. The oath teaches medical ethics.... Apparently.

Kanchinaadham could not communicate with dying mother. A communicative chasm, a language-related rupture continued to subsist between them. She was ancient grief. It needed not be a family affair. Subbamma was the emblem of distress that was integral to countless Brahmin families. Hugging this ancient grief to heart, encrypting many a secret in its compact spaces, Subbamma passed on silently from this world into the Silence of the Universe. That great Silence stayed on in Kanchinaadham as the permanent problem of language. It informed his withdrawn nature – in language, in expression, in behaviour, a shrinking, crippling stutter.

What was the origin of Subbamma's great silence? Why did she decline into the vast silence of death, much before she died? Her grief was not hers, not solely personal. It was the accretion of tears from the many villages of Konaseema. The torrent of grief finally merged in the great ocean of *dukkha*. Then, not even little traces remained.

Brahminism was embroiled in a huge catastrophe. At that juncture mostly women were bruised. There is no balm for those bruises. In course of learning this truth, Subbamma assumed the form of silence. This silence terrorized Kanchinaadham deeply. Subbamma suffered not just her daughter's sorrow;it was the cumulative grief many Brahmin women of the town suffered... secretly. She had one friend… a widow. The widow achieved a pregnancy. Nine months of gestation later, even the family members deigned to recognize it. The unfortunate woman bore extreme insult – beyond words.

Subbamma said – well, it's happened. We cannot change the state of past months. Let's ask a doctor what to do, and she led them to hospital.

Full term pregnancy… "drugs would endanger the host," said the doctor.

"No matter," they said; "family honour is more important."

Result… Stillborn.

The corpse that Kanchinaadham saw in the Mukkamala canal was that very infant. That's how Subbamma drew into herself her personal, and the town's generational grief. It was never possible to separate the two.

One, only one, daughter generated ... dead, or deserted, she did not know. Son, Kanchinaadham's regenerative success in world seemed surely remote. No hope of a bride brought home, an infant's cackle following. Hard-to-tell reasons. She, reasons silenced, lived in an ossified moment of grief. The close-bosom-friend to whom she could unburden herself, had died under unfortunate conditions. They had grown up together, at the same time, in the same period. That woman died in hospital, suffering hellish pangs. Subbamma had to harbour the deathly secret. Many issues she hid in her bowels, *garbha*. Her daughter's life, too. Could not openly sob away. All of it, a carefully protected grief, like a precious pregnancy, like invisible canal waters gurgling soundlessly under the bridge on a dark new-moon night, amniotic fluid inside the cavernous womb. This tense, silent grief led her into epilepsy.

Saambayya Dikshithulu concluded that Subbamma's recurrent epileptic fits were the result of witchcraft. He invited a witch-doctor to cure it, but to little avail. Yet she was cured. At this precise juncture of time, Saambayya Deekshitulu had a disciple, Subrahmanya Sastri. Sastri was learning the Vedas from him. The one who freed Subbamma from epilepsy was Hymavathi, Saambayya Deekshitulu's disciple's wife!

Hymavathi understood Subbamma's silent grief. "Amma! Dukkha has no beginning, no end," she said. The more the recall, the greater the grief. From the well-spring. There may be an end to this town canal; but none for dukkha. *Samsaara,* life of this world, is in essence, dukkha.. "We mothers concieve children, not their karma, actions and fates," consoled Hymavathi. This last utterance gave Subbamma solace, and restored her to health.

Subbamma recalled this utterance throughout her life. We birth children, not their fates; no one can change the writ of the moving finger in the wrinkles of the brow. No one can comfort another in the state of dukkha. These words stabilized her in the state of Sheer Silence, *maha mouna*. Is Silence a sign of sickness or of restoration to health, Kanchinaadham asked himself. Sri Sri had said 'Silence was body's cemetery, not soul's solution.' Shankaraacharya had said *silence was manifest commentary on the nature of the Divine Ultimate.*[5] Kanchinaadham was caught in a conundrum – was Silence the Absolute, *gravitas*, or was it burial, the deep, endless burrowal of death?

Mukkaamala Canal is not silent either. It also has been conversing in its own singular code. At night, in the silence is heard its whisper.

Sound, word, language... how beautiful these are! Speech sustains man. However great the grief, it gets tempered in language. Like earth, grief is also layered. The upper crust is common. As you dig deeper, sorrow leaps at you like dragon flames. The dukkha that constituted the mute chasm between Kanchinaadham and Mother is of the kind.

Kanchinaadham thought – how good, had I been writer. Could I write, I could have escaped this laryngeal torture, asthmatic, fibrotic heaving, the inexplicable sense of sinking into a quicksand, gasping. Adamant Silence, left behind by Mother, could have softened and flowed ... away ... at least some of it. Then he lashed at himself, clipped his thought. He wasn't a man of letters and litters.

He personally knew contemporary writers, thinkers, though. He had studied for some time at Rajahmundry. Also inculcated the habit of reading some contemporary literature. Thought Kanchinaadham, there is no relation between my thought, my torture, and the current literary milieu. Prevalent literary culture is very progressive. Running at some clip on rails. Capable of methodical direction.

3

In Telugu literary milieu the Pragatineni wedding invitation is regarded as a wake-up call. That wedding, asserted intellectuals, was universal celebration of prosperity. The grandeur was the very glory of Telugu literature, they affirmed.

Pillars of modern Telugu poetry praised, trumpet tongued, the marriage mantapa for having lent modern five-star flavours to the ancient language of Telugu. After all, Pragatineni was no commoner! He was modern Telugu literature's manifest patron, Srikrishna Devaraya. Not only did Pragatineni brand and let loose every ones stories and poems among the public, he also gave away grand gold bracelets to all, conferring international celebrity status (Pragatineni adopted this from the practice of branding and releasing bulls raring for a go among cows, a highly creative activity, thereby giving a new meaning to tradition and modernity). Modern Telugu literature was Pragatineni's historical find, asserted intellectuals.

Today is Pragatineni's daughter's wedding. Groom is big businessman in America. Dowry was one crore rupees. The marriage pandal alone cost lakhs. Pragatineni loved accounts in books, certainly, but loved books of account even more. Books accounting dollars were further more dear. Big men aver that in him Lakshmi and Saraswati at last joined hands. Such a towering personality as Pragatineni alone could ensure the internationalization of a Telugu literature that was languishing for lack of patronage.

The pandal shone with such brilliance that Kanchinaadham could not withstand its intense glare.. The light skewered the eyes and needled the brain. The mind was getting benumbed. He had never seen so much light. Such terrible, harsh, hateful light had never dared invade the village Mukkaamala, or the hamlets of Konaseema. So much light! My God! So much light? This is nothing other than darkness visible, *shweta andhakaara,* a searing white blackness, he thought.

In that cruel darkness, Kanchinaadham found an acquaintance, Sarwasvam.

4

Everyone says Sarwasvam is an English quotation. He tells everything in the form of a quotation. Even a simple statement is in the form of a citation. Suppose Sarwasvam had to say, "I'm feeling hungry." He would not directly say so; he wouldn't be Sarwasvam if he did. "Hunger is natural to life, says the French philosopher Robert, "that's why I feel hungry." That's how his sentences are constructed. Sarwasvam does not speak without an English quotation, without citing a reference. It is his firm belief that speaking without an allusion is very insulting to a scholar of his stature, who was constantly engaged with the churnings of Western epistemological world.

However, these allusions flushed Sarwasvam down the drain in some matters. His love-life turned a total travesty. He was loved by a young woman. While engaged in love-making, he sought to make allusions. English allusions, and their translations as well. Vexed with this encyclopedic love-making she deserted him saying "make-love to your stupid quotations, you mindless maniac!" She never even saw his face, leave alone making love to him, again.

Is it time up for quotations? My God! Can I quote so much, if I did not rote through countless English treatises? What have I to do with a girl who has no use for knowledge – meaning quotations? I'll wait eternally for a beautiful quotation, vowed Sarwasvam, virtually tying a ritual-armlet to his wrist as a permanent reminder of the vow.

There is no self interest in his quotationism. He is himself a huge quotation. Each person is born in a special way. The reason could be karma, it could be genetic, who could tell?

Pragatineni introduced Sarwasvam to Kanchinaadham. "Getting a new friend is like finding a new brand of whiskey," said the American intellectual Bo Gus Moon. "That's why meeting you makes me very happy," said Sarwasvam, shaking hands.

Hanumantha Rao, alias Birsa Munda, was also introduced during the hubbub of the marriage. He was born a Brahmin. Parents gave the name Hanumantha Rao. Having assimilated communism and anti-casteism, he changed his name to Birsa Munda, that of a tribal hero.

The marriage venue glowed like another world, illuminated by the leading lights of the time, writers and intelligentsia, literati and glitterati. Writers were engaged in a review of certain progressive trends in literature. The hosts and guests, relatives, were exchanging details of dowries and gifts. Some unnamed nausea rose in Kanchinaadham. Head began to reel. He dashed out fearing a bout of vomiting.

Meanwhile the traditional band of music began. A Tyaagaraja composition on sannaayi, accompanied by the beats of a dhol. The sannaayi breathed an air that ever so slowly released him from the earth.

The sannaayi notes made a soothing mixture of music.

Kanchinaadham felt a little calmed.

The loud critical fuss in that ambience had little sensible to say about the natural form and charm of art. Creation does not bend to critical cavil. Only in some interior ranges of the Himaalayas, without the interference of the allusionist critic's mindless meddling, in the severity of silence and solitude, the natural Shivalinga forms, perfect in itself.

5

Knowledge is my sweetheart, says Sarwasvam. After the lover abandoned him, he has been chanting this repeatedly. He has also been attributing it to some American philosopher, not willing to miss the occasion to allude.

Sarwasvam's pursuit of knowledge is such that he invited it through all his nine orifices, and ninety million pores. In winter he slept, buried under books. All of those were English books.

This is how he propagated the view that 'knowledge' was sensually comforting. English books are printed on smooth, silken, fragrant paper. So they also offer the scope for sensual satisfaction.

Besides, these printed books are selfless. They give pleasure but do not seek pleasure in return. So there is no need to demonstrate potency, ensure sperm-count. Through this device, English capped the world as the imperialist business language. Sarwasvam is only a little worm, honey-trapped by its allure.

Actually, ninty five percent of world languages are only spoken. They have no script. So they have no scriptural sanction and support. Only five percent languages have learnt orthography. These languages have the hegemony of the rest – erasing them out of existence. Of that five percent English has become the language of power over the world. It is a colonial language, hence acquired the status of a communicative tool. Also a means of knowledge. That isn't all; it's now a modern religious belief, a theosophy. A maantric power, excitation issues forth when the language is spoken. To thinkers such as Sarwasvam, it has become central to life, a sexual need. That's why the view has gained strength in them, that everything written in these books is regenerative, sacrosanct. Just as tradition believes that what hasn't passed through the conch is no libation, so Sarwasvam believed firmly that only what has been quoted from or alluded to in Western, English treatises, may aspire to the status of Truth. He was so engorged with western knowledge that without the citing of an English quotation, he could not even achieve an erection. This is what cost him his lady-love.

6

Reading Telugu books leads to the problem of premature ejaculation.

This scientific fact was also discovered by Sarwasvam. Consuming greedily from English, regurgitating it unassimilated, chundering chyme, was the trend of Telugu literature. Telugu story, novel, essay, theory... all... solely a translation of English, nothing else. Been so from the beginning. The intellectual to have recognized this from the first moment was Sarwasvam. He commanded awe and awful servility from Telugu writers. Because he did not read Telugu books. He read only their English originals. That's why he's gained recognition as an original thinker. Discovering the English origins of any given book and citing it, is the sign of original thinking, say elders.

That's why Sarwasvam has classified persons into great ones, who quote all the time from English; common ones, who quote only occasionally; and petty ones, who quote not at all. This classification is accepted by all Telugu literati.

Sarwasvam does not read Telugu books. But he has earned great reputation as a Telugu critic par excellence. He acquired that aura only because he did not read Telugu books.

In fact, Telugu writers have realized that reading their own work is boringly dull. That's the reason why they get rid of them quickly, distributing them free of cost to all. Perceptive readers promptly sell them off by the kilo. Within a month of publication, those masterpieces vanish from the market, and from the hands of the authors and readers as well.

Why would Sarwasvam read such books, either? Writers themselves wouldn't respect him, if he did. He would attend the book-release function without having read the book. Ask the author sitting next to him what was in the book. The author usually mumbled two bits. He would then ask the author to reveal the name of the original. Next moment he got to work, weaving a smooth fabric of a speech. This fabric was a weave of quotations.

This ability to weave a thick fabric of quotations earned him recognition as an Original Mind.

It is an indisputable fact that Sarwasvam did not read Telugu books. But in case of inevitability he read their English translations; because he had fully understood that translation is an independent text.

Translators write what they fancy as an English book. To that they handcuff a Telugu writer's name. To be true, these translators, too, do not read the Telugu texts. In fact they have won acclaim as accomplished translators precisely because they have not read Telugu texts. In any case the original to the Telugu text has already been English. Make a few changes and christen it a translation!

That's how they become translators of vintage originality.

Gradually Sarwasvam stopped reading translations also. He'd learn directly from the author the source of his thoughts, story and techniques. He'd then read up the source text. He is a Telugu critic thus, and an intellectual, one who has altogether disowned Telugu literature. That's how he has won so much honour; that's why he is invited to all international Telugu meets abroad, with such fanfare.

Sarwasvam's impromptu expressive ability is unbridled. He does not fumble for words; because he imports all thought and phrase, by then well-settled in the West. So does he import theories and technical terms; he does not needlessly waste time and intelligence teasing after original thought.

This is the secret of his fluent expressiveness.

7

Kanchinaadham is impotent – said Doctor Bhagawantham.

It was Pragatineni's magnificient manor. Hanumantha Rao alias Birsa Munda, Sarwasvam, Pragatineni and Doctor Bhagawantham had assembled there... lovers of literature.

Doctor Bhagawantham was a renowned sexologist from Vijayawada, who had also produced a popular pragramme on sex for the television. His book *Kavula Sex Samasyalu* (*Sex: Poets' Problems*) was a lasting chart-buster.

Kanchinaadham was one of Bhagawantham's patients.

Actually Kanchinaadham's private travail hadn't much potential for public interest, because he was not a man of name and prestige. Not an intellectual. Indeed he suffered from an unresolved expressive problem. Now there was the added problem, a sexual dysfunctionality. Who was likely to die of curiosity about such a man?

However, his problem raised immense curiosity in them. What reason? One who is always busy in hot pursuit will experience an aversion towards a person who is always inert, lazing on the promontory. There is an element of anxiety, fear that this laid-back Letharge may be stealing a march over the eternal athlete ... in achieving peace.

> Wastefulness wearies the seeker.
> Sloth stops the speedy in his tracks.
> Fruitlessness faults fruitfulness.

Those intellectuals had precisely some such reasons for their curiosity about Kanchinaadham.

The diagnosis that he was impotent made them joyous. Sarwasvam was so much more swollen with joy. "I could not achieve an erection without the foreplay of a juicy English quotation. This Kanchinaadham is altogether lost to the boil of passion. Useless. An uncouth fellow who has turned his back on the Deep, the deeply uterine resource of Western knowledge, A lowly, *kshudra* Brahmin who could not even read the English alphabet; a dunce who could not respond with minimal sensitivity to my brilliant English quotations. Such a fellow's very living is meaningless. God! In your infinite mercy, let him wilt and buckle under the permanent burden of flaccidity," prayed Sarwasvam.

8

Sexologist Bhagawantham suffered from a peculiar sex problem. The doctor addressed sexual problems with tremendous enthusiasm. He derived from his encounter with newer sexual problems, the kind of raw excitement and intense pleasure which the early savage man derived from fierce hunting in the fearsome forests of foregone times. This was his daily routine; if no patient came, no new problems cropped up, he'd be deeply disturbed. He'd crumple and collapse, and wilt under the burden of a sexual dysfunctionality.

Don't ask, what sexual problems can arise every day. Modernity, increasing by the day, has added to the growth of sexual problems. This has acted as an aphrodisiac to Doctor Bhagawantham, sort of an intensifier, awakener, light-giver.

One day a software engineer came to Bhagawantham. His problem was that he'd experience a powerful sexual urge when he sat before a computer; he'd cool off the moment he jumped into bed, switching off the computer – discalm of mind, all passion spent! If he went back to the internet, the juices overflowed in torrents. Meaning, the computer had been translated into his very reflex, the pulse of his passion and life.

Many such problems present themselves to Bhagawantham. The innumerable problems of the modern society translate into poetry and story, and fumble about Pragtineni's Lotus Feet. Pragatineni gives them international currency, translates them into dame-fame and dollars. Likewise, Doctor Bhagawantham translates the innumerable sringaric issues of the modern age into a career.

9

Kanchinaadham went to Doctor Bhagawantham recently. Only a few days ago. Narrated his past.

"Doctor ji," he said, "to me this world is very boring." Without much light and energy, very weak. Impotent. Limp like a used and discarded condom.

Everything passes by without touching me. Senses, mere spectators. Earth rotating rather uselessly. Hemispheres gyrating ineffectually.

"Doctorji, the globe is galling. Body is boring. Mechanical World robs me of enthusiasm. Doctorji, I do not know why I am alive."

Doctor Bhagawantham paced up and down the room. The utterance 'globe is galling' gobbled up him too. Made him tongue-tied. What did it mean?

Kanchinaadham was talking on. "Doctorji! Man looks to squeezing out a little excitement from evil, from forbidden fancies. Forbidden fruit look luscious. He lives by senses rather than reason. His rational feats are all delusion; intellectuality is the complete muff's camouflage.

Doctor Bhagawantham collapsed into his chair. What's he saying ? I know some literature; Pragatineni, the permanent address of literature, is a good friend, too! But this Kanchinaadham fellow's utterances are different; this diseased, dissolute fellow's utterances are staunching the free flow of language and changing its course.

Meanwhile, Kanchinaadham's own words tumbled on regardless. "Doctor ji ! Fear of evil and dread of grief are hounding me like wild brutes. An ancient world's cultural burden is bending me towards the abyss of paataala. Razing down my sexual excitement. Translating my impulses into incomprehensible impotence."

The doctor sighed. Kept mum as if he had stumbled upon himself unwittingly. Then he said, "Look Kanchinaadham... times have changed, world has changed. Science is opening all doors. Peeping into life's minutiae. Exploring genes, mapping the genome. Everything is clarified. World is manifesting itself with clarity and simplicity before the eyes. Past is gone. Only Present exists. But, know what is most amazing of all man's discoveries, one that has translated the world?" He raised the questioning eyebrow like an archer raises arrow to bow; then fell silent again.

You tell me, said Kanchinaadham.

"Condom"...said the doctor. "CondOm".... His lips rounded ... Om, ...Aum..., boomed or silenced, neither knew.

The word resounded in Kanchinaadham's ears throughout the day, Today there is nothing that can control the body. Not culture, not even dreadful disease. CondOmkaara has given body this final release from confinement...

...in a word moksha.

10

Next day Kanchinaadham went to a whorehouse in Peddapuram. There he saw a woman. He was deeply impressed by her beauty. He asked her name.

"Sundari," she said.

Tried to make...

... conversation with her.

"What's your town?"

"I don't know."

"Your parents?"

"I don't know."

After some such questions and replies, she asked...

... "why do you want these details?

Came for Census!"

She burst out laughing. "All here is senses..." she smiled, ...

... "sensuous," she whispered.

How make conversation with a woman who was *sui generis*, a *Swayambhu Linga*? From where begin? For some time no speech, for some more, silence...

"Time's nearly up," she reminded him.

Kanchinaadham did not know what 'time's up' meant. He does not know what it means to say time is over. The one huge charge about Kanchinaadham is that he does not know the value of time, and that he only knows wasting it. She reached for him saying it's getting to be dawn nearly.

Consciousness of time at this juncture? Time has been hunting me everywhere. Value of time has also risen, after all! Everything within time – to be done within specified time. In factories, schools, whorehouses, time is sold, it's a sell out.

Earth, this solar sphere is sickening, *bhoomandala* is boring, he spoke aloud. Sundari did not understand. Why was this uttered? What did it mean? Is he mad?... many such questions promptly began to buzz in her mind.

Kanchinaadham spoke, almost pleaded – Sundari! At least you listen. I will not touch you. You, at least, understand me. I have been suffering from the lack of sexual impulse for a long while. I met a doctor, trying to find the reasons for this problem. After giving me a patient hearing, what the doctor said was, "Modern man has invented many technological marvels. The most significant of all his inventions is this – he waved a condom drawing it from his pocket.

What is its significance?

He answered the question in a rhetorical turn. "Without fear of any disease, without any hesitation, one may have intercourse with anybody, enjoy with anyone – this was the sum and substance of the doctor's assertion, wasn't it?" he asked.

"Yes," said Sundari.

But, what's all this discourse! Is this fellow rather mad? wondered Sundari. Still, the fellow is special, a curio. His distinctiveness is interesting me. His irrelevancy is alluring. Except for simple, robotic, intercourse, who comes into these caverns paying money to merely talk whatever tattle came to his mind? This fellow has; fine, let's listen, thought Sundari.

Kanchinaadham resumed – his conversation boiled over and flowed. Sex has become very easy.This does not mean sexual desire has grown. Much before he found the condom, man found out another thing. That the earth, without our active role, was revolving mechanically round the sun, within specific time-frames. He calculated time and place. He plunged himself in calculations. He reached a point where he could ascertain infinitely small pulse of time, calculate one-hundredths of a second. Calculate, multiply, divide... multiply, divide ... multiply, divide ...tire out, and let time swallow him up.. He began scanning everything with time. Time-consciousness grew. Beyond bounds. Time is fourth dimension, said man; and some more such trash. As the earth shrunk into a little village, as hurry and hustle grew, time swallowed man. He had no time for leisure now. "Sundari! I have been watching you. You have been watching the watch. Prostitutes have been, for long. Those who are so acutely time-conscious, are new-age prostitutes. Time has gobbled poets and artists. Now... prostitutes. Time has swallowed Sringaara; venomous time has stricken sensuality. Time is none other than money. The fourth dimension has been translated into money."

"Man has worshipped earth; measured it; micronized, shrunk, collapsed, crumpled, withered, wilted it ... calculated, evaluated it. Today is there a greater saleable commodity than earth? Earth has been prostituted. Man takes earth at a rate of so much per pinch. He takes her without condoms. Her virginity is whored and vulgarized. Earth is now infected with venereal disease." He panted as the words gushed out.

"I haven't understood a word. Your time is up. Another customer is in queue. You may go," said Sundari.

11

At about the same time that Kanchinaadham was entering the whorehouse, writers assembled at the princely manor of Pragatineni. They were discussing literature and human relations. Pragatineni spoke with eloquence – Is globalization affecting human relations? The cell-phone chimed. Wherefrom, my son? California? How's business?... asked Pragatineni and was instantly engrossed in conversation with the son-in-law.

In the meanwhile Sarwasvam filled the gap with a quotation. "Human Relations are very important" declared American philosopher DickLuck ages ago. Hanumantha Rao alias Birsa Munda chipped in – for human relations to fortify further, there must be a little love of art, said an intellectual. A rare Telugu species. Occasionally a Telugu fellow also utters wise words, clarified Birsa Munda, because the fellow has studied English. A young writer joined the babble – Pragatineni's is true progressivism, that's why he argues for an egalitarian society in which dollars can be had even in remote villages of Rayalaseema.

One juvenile desperately tugged at his hair trying to make sense of the discussion – what is the real meaning of human relations?

Kanchinaadham made his unannounced entry with one clearly enunciated word on his lips – condoms.

Everyone was stunned. Doctor Bhagawantham promptly backed Kanchinaadham, asserting that he was letter-perfect.

Said Doctor Bhagawantham, Not enough attention is being paid to the condom in Telugu literature. If human relations are to continue in a healthy way, condoms are very essential. It is a sad thing that there is no mention of condoms in today's story and poetry...

12

Time for raging regret. Ten at night. Mukunda Reddy stood before a full-length mirror... stood split in two. One in the mirror, one outside. He questioned himself, which of these is false? Night after night, at ten, he experiences this dichotomy. Bhagyanagara or Hyderabad? The city's split history visits everyone.

Mukunda Reddeee! – called Mukunda Reddy. You are a communist. Have strode through dense forests, gun and all. Forsook fear of death; shredded selfishness with sickle. Lived as though socialism was round the corner.

Reddeee! you had no doubts then. Were not troubled by the question, what recourse, Sonia? You peddled a clear message, ward and street. That's past.

Mukunda ... what are you now? Man outside mirror had tears. Reflections rolled down the mirror. Reddy recalled ... 'nor swoon'd nor utter'd cry.'[6] Weep not Mukunda; change is natural; time is invincible. Time, he told himself sadly, has conquered you.

Who are you today, Mukunda Reddyyy? Bourgeois, investor – international currency. How did this happen? How did it take such a turn? What is true, what is false?[7] asked Reddy, without much zest. Past or future? What do they think of you today, Mukunda? Red is now aneamic. Red is Dead, Reddyyy... right? Poets poke pun at that now ... thought Reddy in introspection.

Such review is Mukunda Reddy's daily routine; and it rambles.

❖❖❖

Sarwasvam rumbled in. All well?

How can all be well, Sarwasvam?. My heart is in perpetual conflict – *my seated heart knocks at my ribs, against the use of nature.*[8]

Now, report the newest state[9] – what do they speak of me? Knowing Mukunda Reddy so well, Sarwasvam was eagerly waiting for this querry.

It was in Mukunda Reddy's nature to expect unstinting universal attention. With it, certainly, walks the fear that no one cares what he expects. He doesn't look for praise; criticism is good enough. Derisive laughter was welcome. Indifference is unbearable.... Earth's rotation, incognizant of his existence, frightened him. Thus wrote Reddy in a poem – *I turn the globe with my little finger/that is revolution.* The verse sprang when a banner blew in his sight – 'Reddys born to Govern'.

Mukunda Reddy breathes fire when the caste system is mentioned. He heartily desires and welcomes annihilation of caste. In essence all castes – except his own – should be annihilated. Only his caste should survive, prosper. That's the principle. So he asserts that shudra castes alone are progressive. Reddys, of course, are the standard-bearers. Many are the times when he's said to himself, I am a revolutionary because I was born a Reddy. In me flows the blood of Reddy kings.

But is my time up, like it was time up for the Reddy Rulers? A chill runs through him. This is how his heart oscillates between superiority and abysmal inferiority.

So he asked Sarwasvam the question again – "Is anyone talking about me? That poet... who's he? ... wrote 'greying gun' – was it about me?"

Sarwasvam said, "Reddy gaaru, no one has the time or patience to bother about another. Each stands before his own mirror, and each views his own face."

"Each one loves himself. Each one sees his own form and masturbates over it, turbation without ejaculation. Reproduction is amoebic – splitting images in magic mirrors. All are split into puns."

"Reddy gaaruu," continued Sarwasam, "I encountered an irrelevancy. Name is Kanchinaadham. Can not put together a single clear utterance. Speaks with a stammer. Is asphyxiated by the perpetual problem of language. Doctor Bhagawantham has diagnosed him. He is convinced that Kanchinaadham is impotent."

Interrupting him, Reddy asked – "Why are you telling me now, about such a worthless man?"

He is worthless, yes; "Most useless of all in the world. He does not know words. He's more worthless than the wordless; meaner than a mute. He is impotent. But precisely these features are causing an irrational fear. They seem to impel the earth towards cosmic worthlessness. Knowledge, acquired after much struggle is becoming powerless. Power is becoming sterilized" – said Sarwasvam.

13

No one is more sterile and wretched than Kanchinaadham. He is an atheist wretch... said Kaasi *annayya*.

Now, from where does this Kaasi annayya pop up?

He is uncle Chainulu's son. A greatly pious pandit from the holy place Kaashi visited Chainulu's home in Nandampoodi on one auspicious day. The pandit came, having heard much about Chainulu's Vedic scholarship. The holy visitor saw Chainulu's eldest son and promptly pronounced him a most fortunate man blessed greatly by the planets. He is so blessed that he does not have to struggle for a living. The Goddess of Fortune will provide for him. The boy was just ten. Everyone called him Kaasi because the pandit from Kaashi had declared him fortunate.

The utterance of the omniscient Seer from Vaaranaasi struck root in little Kaasi's heart. I am fortunate. Indeed I am Fortune. I need not do any work. Million means for a meal? No need of even one skill, decided Kaasi with more than a touch of obstinacy... like Bheeshma of *Mahaabhaarata*.

He did not learn the alphabet, *akshara*, that which never wastes away. Not even one mantra did he learn to chant from the Shaastras. Did no work. But growing into youth, promptly he was married in accordance with the *Saastras*. Four children were born to Kaasi. They grew all by themselves without his playing any role. Yes, he was a Fortunate man.

Fortune has form. An acre of farmland bequeathed by the parents. But that was not adequate to provide for the family. So the brothers left a portion of income from their lands for his family. That's how the family survived. That's it. Even today Kaasi does not know what it means to step into the paddy field. All is done by the lease-farmer.

Kaasi did not know what it meant to step off the ancient home's promontory. He never looked forward to anything. Never desired anything. What was there to lose or gain for a man who was born fortunate?

This Kaasi annayya stood on the ledge of his home in Nandampoodi, and raised his voice... Kanchinaadham is an atheist wretch, a bloody atheist wretch... he began cursing. The invective gushed on...

Kanchinaadham, who'd just then reached the place, fell to wondering. Was he an atheist? He fell into a dissective mode... what is an atheist? True, he did not perform the funeral rites, *karma kaanda* of his parents. But did that qualify him for the label of atheism? Atheism has its roots in modern empiricism, and the causality introduced by science. But in Kanchinaadham, the ancient, there are no signs of such modern empiricism and causality.

The reasons for his denial of funeral rites was disbelief. A disbelief that had swaddled every aspect of this world. His disbelief had extensively shrouded all kinds of beliefs, theories and Faiths. This had bound into complex knots all his peace of mind, plugged the flow of his language, and stunted his sensuality.

Blind belief excites the senses and passions. If old beliefs die, new ones must be born. Blind belief ensures this. The annihilation of belief itself leaves a terrifying, gaping hole; a vast nothingness impossible to populate because the spirit of rational logic is too blunt an instrument. Such a void contradicts life. Belief averts such disaster.

Kaasi annayya may be inactive. But he has blindly accepted the tradition that comes as a hereditary package. He has kneeled before belief. He's acquiesced to the theory of karma. Precisely this acquiescence smoothened the path of his life. It has flown more smoothly than the Mukkamala canal, and more happily. There was no objective. There was no task to accomplish. There was no place to reach. No destination, nothing to gain, none to lose. He's spent seventy years by now, lounging on the ledge of the ruined house in the Nandampoodi *agrahaaram*. There is a huge banyan tree in front of that ruin. Kaasi annayya is the eldest of the house. That old banyan is Kaasi's elder.

Time has changed. *Kali kaala*, the age of reckoning in the infinity of time, had come... to sternly discipline Kaasi annayya. Raameswaram lambasted Kaasi with the anger of a Duurvaasa muni. Will Kaasi annayya ever learn some wisdom? Will he understand responsibility at least before ... a moment before ... his last breath? He doesn't so much as pass by the farm, how should I bide the bugger?

All this time has somehow been managed. Now our children are growing up, too. I don't like the idea of their rotting like me in this vaidic profession. Getting an English education means much expense. Frankly, why should we leave our farms for Kaasi annayya's use? The shaft was on target. Not a jot of work; a bloody parasite that has thrived on the revenues from others' farms, spat Raameswaram.

Then he coughed to ease the strain in his voice. He proceeded to illustrate how worthless, how inactive Kaasi was.

Just the other day, on *kaarteeka somwara*, Yiragavaram Choudhary gaaru, with immense regard, gave him a mango sapling. Choudhary gaaru got it from some place abroad. Expert scientists with deep insight into genetic technology had created this wondrous hybrid. Raameswaram was beside himself with excitement describing the special features of the mango sapling. Do you know what's special about this plant? You wouldn't have heard about such an extraordinary plant – verily the king of all plants – from any of your ancient puraanic texts, he tempted and teased him. Then he unveiled the glorious secret of the sapling.

"It flowers in all seasons; bears fruit in all seasons!"

God! Groaned Kanchinaadham. Fearsome fruitfulness! Incessant fruitfulness frightened him. Perennial flowering and fruitfulness compelled by modernity made him pensive.

What Raameswaram had done was to bring this perennial hybrid and ask Kaasi to plant it in the farm. Kaasi did not pay heed. He did not as much as glance at it. Finally Rameswaram himself had to plant it. It has already begun to bear fruit. Then – Raameswaram closed the illustration with his caustic comment...

The sapling would be dead had I waited for Kaasi annayya to act.

Then came revile – such a wasteful laggard was Kaasi that he would not take care of this rare sapling!

They strolled towards the farm, then homeward, chatting about this modern technological marvel, the special, hybrid sapling. It was dusk. Kaasi annayya was sitting on the promontory performing the evening rituals of sun-worship. In front, the banyan tree, with its clutch of adventitious roots, stood silent, inert. All of the world was racing towards fruitfulness. The banyan stood fruitless, worthless. Some unknown birds gathered in its thick clumps of leaves, making a cacophony.

14

"Man without a thirst for knowledge is like a tree that bears no fruit, said renowned English intellectual Andrew David ...," began Sarwasvam, a dialogue with an obligatory quotation. It was the hospital. He sat before Bhagawantham.

Sarwasvam continued – I have read books from different countries. All of Europe's philosophy and literature is cached in my mind. Western knowledge is ingrained in every ion of my being and body. I am a computer, a walking encyclopaedia, a machine that pops an English name each second. Telugu intellectuals believe that their lives are blessed if only I uttered their names once. They hope that at least a little of the Authority of Western intellectuals will accrue to them if I, Sarwasvam, cited their name in some context. I am a black-skinned white sahib. I am English in the robes of Telugu.

I am an imported tree that flowers and fruits perenially. I am a hybrid *kokila* that sings in all seasons. My mental powers, he raved, are so great... he panted a while and rested to recover his breath. Then he drew his chair closer to Doctor Bhagawantham. "Doctor ji," he spoke haltingly, my mental powers are unlimited... but my sexual ...," he trailed off.

"Don't be embarrassed, Sarwasvam gaaru; tell me," encouraged Doctor Bhagawantham, who had a natural predilection for new sexual problems. He egged him on.

"Doctor ji, knowledge itself is turning into a serious road-block for my sexual life. Unless I quote something from English, I don't achieve an erection.

"Insensitive" to my problem, my lover eloped with someone," blubbed Sarwasvam. "With great diligence I acquired much English-knowledge; stuffed my head to bursting with authoritative quotations; I'm not the great devastation Kanchinaadham is. I am an intellectual, leading a life of fruitfulness with the full backing of Western canonical knowledge... doctor ji, how...why does this problem afflict Me...," asked Sarwasvam, balefully.

AEEDS – Acquired Epistemosed Erectile Dysfunctionality Syndrome, diagnosed Doctor Bhagawantham directly. Its chief characteristic is a tendency to erection only when stimulated by knowledge.

"You have alienated your body. Your lover taught you this truth ... rather cruelly. She is the Tree of knowledge, *Bodhi Tree.* You must recognize one truth. Sexuality does not spring from citation; Sringaara surges from excitation. It is not a quotation you may thrust on a passive audience. It is not a recitation of poetry or story. Like it or not, we applaud when a man of high designation quotes or recites. A vice-chancellor commands admiration; a politician compels astonishment. Deception is possible in the pursuit of the intellectual and the epistemological. But the body cannot, will not deceive...nor be deceived. Sex is body's language. It does not quote from authorities, it speaks *suo motu*. You may deceive with language. You can not deceive with body. Impossible."

Forced by habit, Sarwasvam let out another quotation – "Prominent English intellectual Andrew David said in *Body and Knowledge* that Body is a tree and knowledge is its fruit."

Furious, Bhagawantham warned sternly: Bury this useless knowledge in a deep trench. It is this knowledge that's muddled up your life. It has transformed your body into a lifeless trunk.

What you term knowledge is nothing but colonial Christian knowledge. What does it propagate? *Sringaara* is evil, sex is mean, sensuality is sin, uncivil, primally savage, beastly. That's why one must overcome the impulse. Isn't this the juicy essence? Employing this standard, colonial Christians tarnished and trashed the literatures, sculpture and arts of this country. Intellectuals and reformists here took these ideas to heart and fell prey to a low self-esteem. They became ashamed, apologetic, of their own culture and impulse, said Doctor Bhagawantham.

Not true. Our horizons have broadened, our minds are liberal, solely due to this colonial knowledge, retorted Sarwasvam, joining issue.

What's this liberalism? Is it the rejection of everything by measuring against a colonial standard? Are their standards unquestionable? ... Challenged Bhagawantham. Then he proceeded to elaborate the grave harm done by colonial attitudes.

With the firm belief that sringaara was sin, the colonial labelled SriKrishna Leela as sinful. Proscribed Muddu Palani's *Raadhikaa Saantwanam*, because it dwelt in sensuous detail on Sri Krishna's sringaaric behaviour. Similarly, banned treatises such as *Taara Sasaankam* on the ground that they gave descriptions of unbridled carnality. Such attitudes translated Sringaara into something illegitimate.

Sarwasvam quoted again... "Sringaara was considered sinful even in the Bharatakhanda according to an English intellectual, Kwik Duck." Sarwasvam held up the *sanyaasa aasrama* as the definitive example illustrative of this attitude. But Doctor Bhagawantham disputed this. Paramahamsa Shankaraachaarya, the abstemious mendicant, also learnt the *Kaama Shaastra*; learnt by practice. Employing his skill in transmigration, he entered the dead body of the king Amaruka, and cohabited with the king's consorts. Mastered the art of sringaara.

Subsequently, he also authored *The Kaama Shaastra*. This story is narrated in the treatise *Sankara Vijaya*. What does it illustrate? Its essence is that even the most knowledgeable *Brahma Jnaanis*, too, should not ignore and neglect sringaara. Hence the inclusion of sringaara in the four desirable kinds of human activity, Chaturvidha Purushaartha. Hence the description of sringaara as the twin of *Brahmaananda*, the immeasureable joy of being the *Brahman*. That is why Bhoja asserted that sringaara is the sole underpinning, the principle of *rasa*. We do not subscribe to the view that *kaama* is Sin; that is colonial Christianity for you, said Bhagawantham.

Sarwasvam expressed his skepticism... "then why do we condemn Muddu Palani's poetry about Sri Krishna's sringaara?"

Colonial education and culture led reformists and intellectuals into believing that kaama, sensual desire, was sinful, aboriginal, primitive, uncivilized, explained Bhagawantham. "The opacious concept of Original Sin clouded the subcontinent with a blindness from which recovery seems remote", he countered.

Sarwasvam accused Bhagawantham of laying the entire blame at the door of the colonial.

No. There are many historical facts in evidence supporting what I say. The colonials rejected as uncivilized all of our culture, literature, arts, beliefs, traditions, stories and narratives. Termed them primitive; sinful. There was much too much, they said, of untrammelled description of ex-marital sringara in them; and there was no ethic. And they banned these works. Actually a sense of exclusion, a ban, does not inhere in *sanaatanam*. That was imported by the colonials – said Bhagawantham.

"How can you tell that colonials have an influence on our intellectuals?" questioned Sarwasvam aggressively.

Bhagawantham doggedly dinned on – the very foundation and basis of our current intellectual life is colonialism.

Sarwasvam expressed his vexation with dogmatic allegations. There must be supporting evidence, an authority for every utterance.

Intellectuals and reformists, and Hindu ideologues mushroomed under the influence of colonial Christianity. The founder of the Arya Samaaj, Dayananda Saraswati, is hailed as India's Martin Luther. For the simple reason that he was the Hindu intellectual who gave colonial Christianity a local name and habitation. Dayananda Saraswati rejected the *Bhaagawatam* as replete with immorality and sin. The vivid descriptions of Sri Krishna's *sringaara kreeda*, sensuous play, were the cause of his violent anger. His strong revulsion owed to the colonial Christian concept of the Original Sin. He considered the luscious descriptions of Sri Krishna's *madhura sringaara* – sweet sensuousness – utterly, viciously sinful. Indeed he dared to insist with an ignorant courage that *Srimad Bhaagawatham* be banned. Can there be a greater tragedy ?... sighed Bhagawantham, sadly.

Sarwasvam dismissed it all as a hundred-year old history. All progressive thinkers raised Muddu Palani to high heavens. They applauded her gutsy expressive ability. Christian colonial education enhanced their liberalism, said Sarwasvam.

No, no. Not at all. From reformists to communists, all were trapped by a Christian Sin-syndrome. A pusillanimous inferiority, a wilting of the soul, a spiritual cringe cribb'd, cabin'd and confin'd them...blared Bhagawantham.

On what authority do you assert this?... steamed Sarwasvam.

Why authority? Can be understood from watching our communists and progressive writers today. From the way they censor their ideas and writings...

See! You can not cite authorities. You have little historical perception, and less back-up research, argued Sarwasvam.

Bhagawantham countered with passion – You do not see the obvious. Experience is not enough for you. You live in the delusory world of the written word.

The Book is greater than Experience. The Written alone is the Truth...screamed Sarwasvam.

That is the origin of your sexual dysfunction, said Bhagawantham. New ideologues, flush with Christian sense of sin, cast the heavy burden of graphic bestiality on the easeful eroticism and sensuality of adventurously liberal writers such as Muddu Palani. They termed this age of *sringara pradhaana prabandha kaavya* an age of decay and degeneration. Know what K.V. Ramana Reddy, the renowned Communist critic said about Muddu Palani? That she wrote more vividly obscene sringaara than any male writer had, untrammelled by natural feminine circumspection and delicacy. He faulted her for writing about non-marital sex; criticized it as immoral; condemned it as uncivil.

But, went on Bhagawantham, in *Sanaatana Dharma* sexuality is neither uncivil, bestial, nor immoral. Free, unrestrained love has been portrayed with vivid exuberance in our *Puraana* and *Prabandha Kaavyaas*. Sringaara is said to be the path of *moksha*, the release from the cycles of birth. It is Christian education that first introduced the view that sringaara is sin. In the modern age this led to the belief that sringaara is contrary to progress. It is with such a world view that sringaara was treated as taboo and banished from Progressive and Revolutionary Writings. Sex stood censored. Only one writer, a *Sanaatanist*, interrogated this concept of sin, said Bhagawantham.

Sarwasvam sought to know the name of this venerable writer.

Gudipati Venkatachalam... replied Bhagawantham calmly. Chalam stood bold ground against the onslaught of this Christian sense of sin, armed with the sword of the Sanaathanam. Whether sringaara was labelled blatantly obscene, or benightedly bourgeois, he was determined to write only sringaara. His declarations comprise the very essence of Sanaatanam... said Bhagawantham.

Sarwasvam raised one more objection. Many Puraanic narratives tell of the *rishis*, holy men, who went into deep and long meditations to overcome the sringaaric impulse. What do you have to say about that?

The Bhagavad Gita teaches that the senses more than the body, the mind more than the senses, the soul more than the mind, are progressively abstract and sublime. To arrive at the sublime from the relatively material, one has to journey from the manifest to the unmanifest, from the expressed to the ineffable. There is no rejection of the corporeal, the bodily in this view – said Bhagawantham. This is why great poets have described the sringaara of their most loved and deified gods without the slightest hesitation or constraint. Kaalıdaasa described the sensuous love of Paarvati and Parameswara in *Kumaara Sambhavam*. Bhakti poets described the unending sringaaric indulgence, *raasa leela* of Sri Krishna with free abandon. Meaning, gods are not beyond the scope of Sringaara, the play of Creation, said Bhagawantham.

You speak lies. You've gone blind to the facts ranging before your eyes. If what you say is true, why have Hindus destroyed nude paintings of gods? Asked Sarwasvam

Hindus are none but the hybrid twin of the Christian. Follows that the attack on nude paintings is naught but an attack on sanaatanam. One must search through the *Garuda Puraana* to find suitable punishment for such crime... spoke Doctor Bhagawantham.

To analyse and understand these Puraanaas, Shastras, Vedas, one must know methodology. That is the forte of the Englishman. Frankly, we know nothing of methodology, said Sarwasvam.

Erections can not be achieved through theory and methodology! You consign all your treatises to flames and fill your room with blue movies. There is no other cure for your problem ...finished Bhagawantham's frenetic discourse.

15

Moods don't materialize out of methodology; precepts don't precipitate performative impulses. Rasa can not be realized through rote or readings... asserted Doctor Bhagawantham. It was a moonlit night, on the banks of the river Krishna.

Sarwasvam, Pragatineni, Hanumantha Rao alias Birsa Munda and other intellectuals were engaged in a literary discussion with Bhagawantham.

Doctorji, said Pragatineni...you are by nature a very modern man. Somehow, in recent times, there is a marked change in your thoughts.

True. Bhagawantham had observed something new about himself. While analyzing Kanchinaadham's case, he realized the futility of examining sringaara in a space exclusive of local culture and traditions. The literary perceptions of India must be examined within local parameters, not by colonial metrologies.

Alamkaara Saastra describes the ecstasy of joy arising out of poetry as the non-dualism of Advaita, a unified experience that erases boundaries and blends the apparently immiscible.

Not an objective, distant standpoint and analysis, but an amalgamation in the very stuff of poesy. It is a state in which knowing and the known, perceiver and the perceivable are integral; difference is cognitive, not perceptual. That is the Emotive Joy, a dwelling in *Rasaananda*, from the engagement with the poem.

Standing afar, retaining ones special state as viewer, and analyzing as a judge is the colonial way. That is not our method. Colonials, retaining distinctiveness, without surrendering to the One, maintaining intellectual untouchability, criticized our arts and literatures. Expressed their judgements, passed verdicts. We are blindly conferring on this methodology a divine status. That is the origin of our impotency, said Bhagawantham.

16

Sarwasvam vanished without trace. Why, and where he went, no one knew. A lock hung on his door.

Intellectuals virtually went mad missing his quotations.

Long later, a letter reached Bhagawantham. It was from Sarwasvam.

Doctor Bhagawantham gaaru,

My eternal gratitude to you for freeing me from knowledge. My body has earned salvation. Senses have begun feeling light enough to fly. Existence, rather than social success, is the essence. Knowledge is futile, analysis is futile. I lived gorging on and purging publications. There is nothing to books.

Body is ancient. It is a tree that draws upon water and air, and gives oxygen. I burdened and bent it with loads of alien knowledge. I banished myself from our ancient wisdom, sayings, traditions, utterances and greetings. Settled into the role of a consumer of the spectrum of Western knowledge markets. Brought impotence upon myself.

Our Telugu colonial intellectuals and writers raised my impotence to the level of ontic uniqueness and flattered me. Translated me into an exporter of their wares. Now the Telugu country is England. I am now at a safe distance from it, in a small hamlet in Assam. It's a happy life. No more do I dribble quotations nor spew English names. No more do I import Western knowledge. Don't give my address to anyone, please. I have exited the dreadful colonial intellectual world. Goodbye.

Thank you for rekindling the sexual impulse in me.

17

It is the tiled house of Dhoolipaala at Mukkaamala. The young woman stood on the promontory and declared that Lord Venkateswara Himself married her. Kanchinaadham was in the crowd that had gathered there.

The girl kept insisting that the marriage took place in a divine dream at midnight. The Divine trinity of Brahma, Vishnu and Maheswara had given their blessings. Her father was trying to send her in, thundering "are you mad! You..."

This is sheer superstition. What the hell is marriage with God? asked one believer in logic, science and rationalism. This rationalist named the behaviour as schizophrenia, and went about explaining its features: seeing things, hearing things, living in an illusion. One vedantin observed that the whole world is an illusion, mistaking rope for snake, *rajju sarpa bhraanti*. A smaller illusion in that great illusion. One skeptic remarked that one couldn't even see God in this Kaliyuga, where was the question of marrying him? Another *bhakta* countered: Wasn't it Kaliyuga when Sri Krishna married Meera Bai? Venkateswara Swami is the chief God of Kaliyuga. What is so amazing about the young woman becoming his consort! Very simple, surely!

While they conversed, the girl's father sickened with his grief. Just the other day her marriage was fixed; an American match. And now she wallows in this madness!

Pragatineni's daughter's wedding came immediately to Kanchinaadham's mind. It was a grand marriage, with lots of money spent on display. It was a display of wealth and ostentation. Is this mad young woman teaching quite the contrary

– that real sringara is living in an imaginary, mythic state, an oneiric state untouched by debasing reality?

Weddings in dreams are not new. Kanchinaadham recalled a story from *Kathaa Saritsaagara.*

An artist gave a wonderful painting as a gift to King Vikramaarka. The emperor was simply stunned by the divinely beauteous woman in the painting. He took wing in a dream romance. He married her in an erotic dream while in a deep slumber. At exactly the same time, the painted beauty in an imaginary island also had a dream. King Vikramaarka appeared in the dream. Promptly she fell in love with him, and took him for her lover. That was dream love, dreamt wedding, dreamy love-making.

A dreamer experiences sensual pulsation, intensation and libidinal satisfaction in the excitement of dream imagination. Great seer – composers did not much like bringing their dreams down to earthly reality. That's why they danced, swayed and sang with inspiration of sublime love, mystic songs that amazed the muses as well as men. Real sensuality, sringaara, is only in the warmth of visions.

Lovely songs and great poems happen in dreams; ravishing romances happen in dreams. What happens when dreams are brought down to earth? What, if Devadas and Paarvati were to get married? Love would dissolve in a moment. Whatever is heated to a boil, simply evaporates in bubbles.

The heart begins its search of new love the moment the present lover is won. That's why imagining a stranger in bed turns love-making excitingly passionate. Whatever comes to hand loses its dream-like quality. What touches the soil is no song, no poetry. Ideals and dreams destroy themselves when institutionalized. Commerce has clipped the wings of dreams and grounded them, globally, thought Kanchinaadham.

18

Birsa Munda, alias Hanumantha Rao, wrote an elegy on an unfortunate woman he had dug into a deep hole, said Sarma. Kanchinaadham, who had met him at a bar in Amalapuram, expressed his amazement. Sarma confirmed that this was on everyone's tongue.

Pragatineni extended his support to Birsa Munda on grounds that he was human, too, prone to weaknesses, not withstanding all his idealism, just as the moon too had its black spots. He showed the way to expiation by suggesting immediate and ruthlessly clinical introspection. Then added that some delay was no mar so long as there was self-examination.

True enough... agreed Sarma and recounted instances. Sometimes, he said, communists indulge in self-criticism years after events. Immediate introspection and self-criticism was not possible when a young woman hoping to join the party was killed on suspicion that she was an informer; or when a train was set ablaze as public protest. Years later, under compulsion of circumstances they subjected themselves to reflexive scrutiny, a self-crticism. Better later than never for such soul-searching, felt Sarma. Pragatineni had no hesitation in seconding the view.

Pragatineni then referred to another phenomenon in this context. Some Maoists declare their mortal opposition to a culture of trade. They desire the death of colonialism. Yet, they were now accumulating wealth with both hands through the businesses of education, real estate and cinema. They seem to have postponed introspection for the present. After some years of successful pursuit of wealth, they would give themselves up to self-examination ...where is the loss? asked Pragatineni.

Introspection has become an inevitable ritual for every sick fool born as a communist, replied Sarma. Proponents of Hindutva, and members of many political parties are happily engaged in money-making without experiencing such duress. If, in the process, there is an accumulation of too much guilt, one could always go to uncle Venkanna's temple at Tirupati and cleanse ones conscience by tonsuring ones head, added Sarma.

Quite right, said Pragatineni. How sad that communists have no god to turn to for making confession and seeking exoneration!

It's all their own making, said Sarma.

Kanchinaadham observed that since they had no god, communists placed themselves in the void so left. This is arrogance in the garb of progress. That girl perished in the encounter with this arrogance.

19

The arrogance of progressivism showed itself starkly in Hanumantha Rao alias Birsa Munda. From childhood, he had grown amidst proponents of rationalism. Atheism was his ambience. Progressivism was his pulse.

When he was barely ten, Birsa Munda took on a wager with his friends. I'll kick the statue of Mother Goddess; nothing will happen to me, he boasted. I'll demonstrate my godlessness in this way, he said. The other children warned him that he'd lose his eyes, and that such an act would bring disaster. But he Birsa Munda went ahead and proved his point. He did the unspeakable to the statue of the Mother Goddess.

It is true that he did not go blind, but owing to Her anger he turned stony. When he walked it looked like a statue walking. His language also hardened. His perception lost the sensitivity and touch of experience. His stony presence was enough to encrust the creative impulse in poets. Lyric turned rock hard. Singers were struck dumb. Music turned mute. His speech, arrogant without parallel, silenced others into eternal aphasia.

It is the curse of the Goddess. Whatever he touches petrifies, breeze becomes boulder. He can not escape from the curse. It was this curse that led the unfortunate young woman to death.

He climbed the mountain peak with her. Some say he pushed her off the peak. Others maintain that she jumped into the abyss herself. Yet others ask, what's the difference. Question is, why did she die? That death is a mystery. Pragatineni says it is now past, it is history. History always goes forward. This is the inexorable cyclicality of history…the curse.

Police official, Krishna Sastri, was an admirer of Birsa Munda's writings.

Birsa Munda's rationalist expression always led to contrary results. His creed also turned into a curse for him. In his revolutionary thought always lurked an anti-revolutionism. That's how the government came to declare an award for his revolutionary writings. Several officials admired his writings immensely. Prime among them was the police-intellectual, Krishna Sastri.

Krishna Sastri's real name was not Krishna Sastri. He was a great lover of the Telugu Romantic poet Krishna Sastri. That's how the name stuck to him. Once, Krishna Sastri was walking around in the forest, deeply impressed by its beauty. He had a sweet voice, and he broke out in song, watching ancient trees, pretty plumes, happy hares.

The song went soothingly – leaf among tender leaves/ blossom among balmy bowers/ downy soft sepal / may I snugly conceal, infuse myself softly in this, thy forest?[10]

Police involved in combing operations at that time were also quite affected by the song. They turned into motionless figures and concealed themselves in the forest. Hours later the spell petered and birds flew helter-skelter. Animals ran amok. Four youths died.

Krishna Sastri's eyes moistened. He is unreservedly and totally averse to violence. The need for using bullets to kill human beings always made him agonize in the extreme.

It was the time when Radical Students' Movement rose to high-tide in the State. Wherever young men bit the dust caught in crossfire, Krishna Sastri was found, maudlin and weeping copiously. The police were astonished. One police officer, a colleague, took him to task for the sympathetic tears he shed. Is there any sense in your behaviour? Why do you weep for wayward young men who challenge the system itself?

True, they have lost their way. Does that mean, countered Krishna Sastri, that they be killed?

What else may be done, then? Are you preaching at us ... like the civil liberties fellows with their desultory rant? asked angry police. They reminded him that the police too were living beings like the Naxalites. Do not weep for the lawless youth, weep for the precious lives of the police, they advised.

Everything you say is quite true, said Krishna Sastri, agreeing with his police colleagues. But our attempt should be to bring wayward youth back into the mainstream. Violence is not a sufficient strategy for this purpose. Violence and counter-violence only lead to the discomposure of the rich and the politically powerful classes, reminded Krishna Sastri.

Then how should the youth be suppressed?

Krishna Sastri replied,: Peacefully suppressed.

What is peaceful suppression?... one policeman wondered. Were suppression and peace not a contradiction of terms?

What appear contradictory are not necessarily contradictions. They meet and merge, philosophized Krishna Sastri. He went on to illustrating it.

Recently I was invited by a private residential school to be chief-guest at the Annual Day Celebrations. I was very impressed by the ambience of the school. Students there were closeted in breathless conditions. The school founder told me that study was the only activity there, nothing else. From dawn to late hours, 11 pm, only study. Song, play, story-telling, idle tattle were all banned and banished. We do not waste time in such trivialities. We tie them up in tough knots of discipline. We are the guiding lights in regimentation, even to the police, asserted the school-businessman, proudly.

Inertia is always dangerous, said Krishna Sastri. That is the root of all revolution, rebellion's soil, seed of ideals and utopias. At least now, do you understand? Is it clear to you now how to eradicate the rash of young generation without wasting bullets? I grew aware of my enjoined duty after seeing that school. Society and State, especially the young generation, should be rid of inertia, aimlessness. Must be translated into a busy-busy state, hard-pressed for time and leisure. Must be subjected to a despotic regime of education from childhood, even infancy. Drown the foetal brain in frenetic activity if technologically possible. Damage the brains, demolish, under the pretext of education. Drain out the grey matter.

Make a generation of sapless, arid, impotent youth. No work for laathiis, understand? If you can morph a generation into stoned youth, no work for laathiis, understand! No need of bullets! No need for violence, explained Krishna Sastri dramatically, the essence of non-violence. Then he reiterated – Easure of inertia is the mantra. Erasure of inertia is the mantra, echoed the hallowed portals of officialdom.

Who is to undertake this grave responsibility? it murmured through one policeman.

The wealthy must establish schools and colleges. Must translate education ino plain business. Introduce perfect competition. Students must feel eternally tense, as if facing death in the battle-field. At-tension, always. If a tender plant cannot bend, can a grown tree bow? asked Krishna Sastri. Root out inertia; exterminate aimlessness. Bend the plant to the desired direction.

Krishna Sastri was a seer, an intellectual who predicted the future. As if to fulfil his vision, private, residential schools mushroomed in each little town. Children could barely find time for ablutions in this business. Regurgitation was all.

Many young men and young women gave up their lives at the altar of the stern goddess of studies (Saraswati seldom smiles on the sleepy!).

The police closed all those cases since these martyrs left suicide-notes declaring no one was responsible for their deaths. Inertia had responded well to the exit-policy. The policy-vision of Krishna Sastri succeeded. Information was being gathered assiduously everywhere. Young folk had little time to stop and breathe, kiss, laugh or love. Skill and study pursued them. Exhausted by the relentless pursuit, young minds found some relief at internet cafes, watching x-age-rated video-clips.

In this atmosphere the nature of intellectuals also changed much. In the age of liberalization, revolutionary ideologues also became liberalized. They acquired properties. Revelled in real-estate. Stumbled after cinemas. Founded private educational houses. Revolution became their part-time occupation. Found reassurance in the thought that they were serving public good.

Hanumantha Rao, alias Birsa Munda emerged from this ambience.

He wrote articles about revolutionary administrations into its own contradiction. All his blessings were turning into curses. God's curse is cruellest. God blest; it curst. Accurst.

20

Kanchinaadham is also accurst. In childhood once he caused coitus interruptus to two great serpents. Thus sacrileged, the sacred serpents cursed him. At the same time, however, they pronounced the antidote in Naagabhaasha, the language of the serpents. Unaware of the language, he could not know it. Indeed, how are we to imagine that he could have understood the thoughts of those divine serpents, when we know that he lacks a primary knowledge of human language? After all, he was a confirmed dyslexic!

In an impotent, useless, inexpressive, dyslexic... you wouldn't expect it. But...

In Kanchinaadham's life, too, there is rasa. There is a love-story in him. Saroja is Dattatreyudu's daughter. Dattatreyudu is Saambayya Deekshitulu's disciple. Their hometown, too, is Mukkaamala. Dattatreyudu's family is a rigidly orthodox family. Rigid to the extent of cleansing burning coals with water. They were unaware even, of marriage after puberty. Married off both daughters in childhood.

Saroja's husband used to study the Vedas in the Vedic school at Kapileswarapuram. Seeing Saroja, Kanchinaadham thought of her as a royal swan. One day he said it aloud – you are a royal swan. Flown in from the snows somewhere in the Himalayas. After a pause, he added, have come for me. She smiled a little.

Was he crossing the limits? She's a married young woman, he'd warn his heart. Saroja would willingly join conversation with him. Sometimes on some pretext, she'd touch him. Extreme orthodoxy leads to extreme libertinism. Waves slap repeatedly on strong shores.

Saroja's husband died in a road mishap. Her grief knew no bounds. But even that grief gradually abated.

Saying that the world has changed is a flaw of language. Many worlds exist in the world. In a changing world there is also a world that staunchly resists change. Dattatreyudu's house is such a yogic state of resistance, Hathayoga.

Into that ancient state, Kanchinaadham stepped every day. Would converse with Saroja.he is neither past nor present, nor change nor accretion. He is challenge... so realized Saroja.

Why did she like him? Indeed, did she really like him? Pity him? Took for a temporary emotional peg? Difficult to tell.

Kanchinaadham was a lost soul. Vestigial evidence of ancient angst.

This very trace transformed him into a stammered expression, a sexual stammer.

One day, Saroja expressed her anguish to Kanchinaadham in a moment of solitude. Said she had lost much by having been married off in childhood. It would have been better had I studied, and been mature. Now he is dead. I have no support, she said, eyes moistening. Our house, in its Hathayoga, stands untouched by change – she lamented.

Really? He gazed keenly at the ceiling and then the walls. It was an ancient tiled-roof house. The beams seemmed very old, he observed.

Yes, they are ancient. Vyaaghreswaram Zamindar gave them to my grandfather. More than sixty years have passed since. But these beams are very strong; will not split easily, said Saroja.

There is change even in your house, said Kanchinaadham, with a roving eye. These electric lights, this stone–floor, and deeper inside, some unknown form of change is insinuating itself into this house. At that moment he looked like a scientist unveiling some invisible elemental properties. You are appearing like the signs of change; the glow of your being has not dimmed despite the deep tragedy that has befallen you, he said, exploring the depths of her eyes. Your lovely hair is like the dark solitude of the new-moon night; I want to bury my face in that dense darkness.

Bounds were breached a little. That brought about a sudden and intense change in the very form of that house. Saroja was silent. That brought him boldness. Your charm is disturbing me as always, he said. The eventime laughed knowingly, merrily.

Gradually there emerged between them the solitude that defines relations of men and women. Why have you stayed single, asked Saroja. Kanchinaadham countered – Who, in this world, is not alone? It touched a deep chord. True, loneliness is not erased by marriage, agreed Saroja. Marriage does not offer such guarantees. Marriage is only a social act, indeed solely a social act. I am not talking of marriage, said Saroja.

Neither am I, replied Kanchinaadham. Saroja… I don't know what you are thinking about me. We have our views about individuals. I have decided to face the world in its reality. Have decided to unshackle myself from the bonds of ancient grief and live in the present alone.

Are you really living the present? – she enquired. We only imagine we are… no one can live like that, she dismissed the thought.

I am determined to view the body only as a body. Am determined to release it from culture and the burden of the past.

I have believed that there is salvation in such action – Kanchinaadham offered a definition of the principle. That's why I went to a whore-house (he decided not to keep anything secret from her).

Saroja said, all right, no need to elaborate these things. Let me live in my imagination of you. I don't want reality. You don't need it either. The world goes round in dreams. It is creating various spheres of illusion for itself. Whores are not just flesh; they, too, are part of culture; they, too, are ancient grief. Who knows how long this canal has been flowing? No one knows what effluents have merged in this flow. It is flowing; it is called flow; that's it. These whore-houses have been there from time without origin. Piety and impiety, purity and impurity are flowing in frictious rub. Everyone knows this. Great sages' hearts have been disturbed many times. Strange men have broken into the stories of fiercely loyal, pious wives. So there is no consistency in our puraanaas. Consistency is impossible.

Why, Kanchinaadham, do you prod meanness in the name of reality? ... anger and annoyance resonated in her voice.

Everyone knows how much lowness, meanness and demonality exist in the world; and knows how real they are. So what? I have understood why you have remained a question mark. Understood why your form moves so leadenly. Understood why you have no friends or dear ones. The flaw is entirely manifest in you, in your very nature... she chastised him.

Kanchinaadham's eyes welled. Past haunts man, he said.

Saroja dismissed his words. There is nothing called past. This world has tasted much tragedy. Now, there are no traces even, ... she said. After this utterance a miracle occurred... or maybe a cataclysm, an earthquake. Saroja slithered forward, held Kanchinaadham's face in her palms and kissed.

21

Lounging on the promontory of the ruined house Kanchinaadham questioned himself. Past, he felt, had dissolved in a flash. That lone kiss had erased all burdensome memories and the secret anguish. Stepped into another world ... it felt. Was all this merely the effect of hormones? Or was there a miracle lodged in Saroja? Why was he making all these analyses? Does any sensible fellow do such things? Excessive rationalism had seeped into him. How and when did this seepage occur ?

22

Kanchinaadham was chewing cud – of his joyous experiences at Mukkaamala village in Konaseema. At about the same time, Pragatineni, Birsa Munda, and other friends assembled at Vijayawada. Birsa Munda said two twos are four. Two twos can never be five, added Pragatineni.

Much have I seen; many countries, and many books. The Book of arithmetical tables is the best of all books. Yes; nothing else has its consistency and conciseness. The principle underpinning man's intellect is a book of tables. Reckoning and assessing everything, multiplying everything, dividing it – these constitute rationality; these alone distinguish us from the animal; these alone liberate us from the past, said Hanumantha Rao alias Birsa Munda.

Only that which is rational is true; that's it. Meaning, everything is transparently clear, simple and assessable, said Pragatineni.

23

It was Mukkaamala. Kanchinaadham was alone with Saroja. Two twos don't make four, said Kanchinaadham.

Saroja laughed and asked, then how much?

Ten, said Kanchinaadham.

They were lying in an embrace on the floor of the ruined-house.

How does two twos make ten? she querried.

Time works differently on earth, and in *swarga*. Now we are in heaven; hours count for seconds here. Earth's maths doesn't hold here.

Then Kanchinaadham said, I have gained wisdom from your shadow.

What wisdom? quizzed Saroja.

Once I used to think that all of earth's burden was on my shoulders. I believed that all of ancient history from the origins of the earth, all of primal grief had ossified around me, he said.

How do you feel now, probed Saroja, peering into his eyes.

Not there any more, no more burden. Each one watches ones own cinema; only, we do it together. There is no satisfying another. Satisfying another is not man's responsibility. In fact, there is no satisfaction. Meetings are incidental, in discharge of ancient debts. I hadn't grasped this. Hence the delusion that I was carrying the entire burden. That bowed and bent me. Now there is nothing that crushes me down, said Kanchinaadham.

How much does two twos make, Kanchinaadham? she asked mischievously.

Complete zero, he replied her with an intense, round kiss.

24

Saroja refused to marry Kanchinaadham. Looking after a family entailed earning a livelihood. Kanchinaadham was not employed. So she gently rejected the proposal.

Saroja's marriage was performed. Not with Kanchinaadham, but with someone else. This marriage created a furore. Dattaatreyudu had performed a second marriage for his daughter. Theirs was a family of strong traditions – always ready for rituals; daily rituals, resonating with Vedic chants; a Sanaatanist family. Kanchi Shankaraachaarya's first blessings were always theirs. A widow-marriage in such an orthodox family! Kanchinaadham. thought, had my father Saambayya Deekshitulu been alive, his heart would have stopped at the disciple's adventure.

Reform of a bygone age, now made its entry into that ancient house. It wasn't a very new movie, only, got released in the Mukkaamala Touring Talkies now.

Time is quick. Inter-caste marriages got performed in many traditional families. Widow-marriages, too. And with the blessings of parents. It was the same with Saroja's wedding. Dattaatreyudu washed the groom's feet and gave away his daughter, performed Kanyaadaana.

Kanchinaadham watched that rare, invaluable event wondering whether it was dream or reality. Tears welled in his eyes. Was the dream disturbed? No, it was safely lodged in his heart. It retained its dreamy texture, delicate purity, eternally emanating a gentle fragrance.

Saroja introduced her husband to Kanchinaadham.

Today I am filled with much happiness, said Kanchinaadham.

Flowers blooming on earth may wilt; those which bloom in the Heavens don't, said Saroja.

Yes, you are a flower of the Heavens; your husband is very fortunate, replied Kanchinaadham.

Part II

Everything gets transformed
into
its contradiction.
It dissolves into
its other.

– Mao

1

Kanchinaadham crossed the bridge. Crossed the Mukkaamala canal bridge. Really crossed. Crossed with an ease that barely recognized the existence of a bridge at all.

Before now, he walked the bridge, bowed and bent, as if the flow tugged hard at him. All his strength just dissipated when he stepped on the bridge. His stride lazed down, he was consumed by weakness. The canal sucked him down.

That sense of heaviness now left him. He felt a lightness, as if exorcised of some burdensome spirit. Saroja had liberated him from some curse.

There was other kinds of change in him, too. He who joined crowds, even small groups, very hesitantly, almost shrunk by the enormity of the occasion, now strode with enormous confidence into the midst, the very centre of a group, like an unerring arrow swiftly finding its mark. He thrust boldly into the midst of intellectuals like Birsa Munda and Pragatineni discussing deep issues.

The unexpected change in him astonished them. They fell to doubting – is this fellow Kanchinaadham? Then, in their unique style, fell to discussing, little minding him.

2

Maoism is the only real modern thought, declared Hanumantha Rao alias Birsa Munda.

Maosim is not a modern philosophy observed Kanchinaadham; it is the essence of Sanaathanam, ancient wisdom.

Everyone was astounded. Aghast, they cast glances everywhere, trying to locate the source of this disembodied voice. Kanchinaadham... opening his mouth and uttering such an unfamiliar, curious sentence stunned them.

It's always good for a stupid man to be silent, said Birsa Munda angrily.

Let a thousand flowers bloom, believed Mao. There's nothing wrong in listening to this fellow! ...interjected Ajooba.

If one listened, there'd be no end to listening. All would speak as they pleased. A life time would be spent just listening. History won't stop for this endless opinion, said Prgatineni.

There is always a big-ant to lead a line of ants. A meeting has a president. A party has a leader. A sentence has a verb – said Birsa Munda.

Ajooba asked – Which is that ant? Who the president ? What signifies the verb?

Sometimes, said Kanchinaadham, inaction is the better part of action. When action is transformed into mere reflex, when action is fossilized into a restrictive prison, when living without action appears a foolhardy move, when such life itself is a sign of insult; when the action-word, verb, works a whiplash chasing terrified man into wild, animal-flight; when the action-word morphs into opportunism, careerism and realtor-rowdyism; when action presides and leads processions with holy, crusading war-cries; when the word becomes God and avariciously seeks sacrifice, then rejecting action, rebelling against the verb, reverbing word into revolt, mutating world into mutiny, is revolution ... said Kanchinaadham. Defying the verb, he reiterated is Revolution.

Kanchinaadham had stated and affirmed that defying the verbal was revolution! Honoured aimlessness with great dignity. Purpose, he argued, was purposeless.

But the inert was not modern, asserted Pragatineni.

Birsa Munda added his assent to Pragatineni's voice. The inactive wasn't Maoist, either. Maoism teaches relentless action. Colonialism also teaches action. Modernism sprung from colonialism. Maoism is a refined version of colonial modernity. Inertia alienates man from modernity, he asserted.

Kanchinaadham launched another missile. In fact the modern are dead opposed to Maoism. Maoism isn't modern.

Birsa Munda watched him with increasing revulsion. The idiot!

Kanchinaadham proceeded, unconcerned. Proponents of colonial modernity completely opposed Maoism – not modern, not progressive. Not activist, not scientific, not logical, they asserted. Halting its spread – that is revolution.

Birsa Munda interrupted Kanchinaadham. No one said those things, don't bluff your way through. I have read all the works of Western scholars. None substantiates your words.

Take colonial reformists, for example, said Kanchinaadham. If you note their opinions, you'll see that they opposed revolutions led by Mao and others. They believed that progress was possible only through colonial administration.

Caught by surprise, Birsa Munda wondered who these intellectuals were.

Ranade, Ambedkar and other modern intellectuals thought so. What did they say? Maoism and the Chinese Revolution were historical blunders, terrible mistakes. National progress was possible only under foreign rule. Backward people like us can achieve progress only under the close, colonial monitoring of advanced nations such as Britain. Knowledge is the very own property of the English people. We will advance only by the operation of Western imperialism. Independence for us is a curse. If freedom comes, we will die of superstition and backwardness. So we must oppose independence; must defy revolutions. Whether India or China, they can prosper only under alien rule; prosper under Western, colonial, Christian rule. They can develop only by submitting to Imperialism. Can can can... progress, prosper, develop ... under, within, by ... colonialism, imperialism, capitalism...? So we must always and wholeheartedly support British Rule. This is the belief of modern intellectuals, said Kanchinaadham.

Yes, truly, progress came to us due to colonialism, imperialism, affirmed Pragatineni. The Railway came. The English language came. As a result, a nationalist vision came. Modernism came.

Birsa Munda closed it out – Our literature came out of its degenerative state.

3

Maosim was the big hurdle, the huge stumbling block to Progressivists, sensed Kanchinaadham. The Progressivists' intense desire to quickly run the track of modernism baulked in the face of a bullish brute called Maoism.

I am a homegrown thinker, said Mao. With this declaration, the very nature of communism changed. Communism got transformed into an oriental nationalism – shedding its European characteristics like a snake shedding its skin.

Mao's was a Swadeshi nationalistic thought; revolt against slavery. It is this Swadeshi nationalism that informs Mao's thought and practice. It is orientalism.

Mao took flight like a mythical bird in an ancient world. He loved the forests, hills and environs of his country. Ancient icons and an affinity for Nature find extensive expression in his poetry and works. Modern, scientific world glooms at a great distance somewhere at the periphery. He was very fond of ancient lore. We, however, look askance at Puraanas. Progressivists are cautious not to mention such things at all. Kodavatiganti Kutumba Rao, Communist writer, highlights this fact in one of his letters.

Kanchinaadham stepped into a pouraanic world with Mao. In all dualities, one transforms into another; Vishnu transforms into Mohini. An accurst angel transforms into a demon. One thing transforms into its complete other, an antonym. Merges fluently into another. The progressive transforms totally into the regressive.

One element of the binary gets transformed into its complete opposite element. It dissolves in its counter. The dual integrate into the One. This is Maoism; this is Orientalism.

Dissolution of the binaries and the emergence of something totally new – a third factor is Hegelian thought. This is not that. One transforms into the other. That is all. Constantly. Always. That's how Mao explained the mutual transformationality of binaries. This is the essence of oriental thought.

4

Mao does not know English, said Sarwasvam. Some years ago he had declared this to Birsa Munda.

Suddenly this assertion from years earlier echoed in Birsa Munda. His face became livid, turned the colour of dark cloud. This is not a simple assertion. Asserting that someone did not know English was like declaring one dead. Maybe even worse...like saying one had never lived.

He recalled the conversation. If Mao did not know English, how did he embark upon the Long-March across hundreds of miles of hills and rocky terrain? How did he direct the revolution? Birsa Munda became motionless for a moment.

Sarwasvam had continued regardless. Mao did not know English. He knew only that wretched, scrambled, God-forsaken cackle, Chinese, he had asserted, thumping the table.

What if Mao did not know English? He wasn't a clerk in a multinational company! An irritated Birsa Munda countered.

Sarwasvam was equal to the task. What is communism without English? Is that within reach of your imagination? Communism was born in Europe. It was born of European sciences. It was born of Europe's modernity. How would a chap without some alphabet understand it?

That fellow Mao was a country bumpkin. Knew nothing more than tilling land and planting saplings. Did not know as much as the value of modern education. Did not know modern methodology. Where would one rank Marx who had a Ph.D from a European university? And where a Mao, who knew not a pen from a ploughshare? That is why, envious Mao shut down all universities. If so much as mildly provoked, he broke into Chinese mythology, Taoism, dipping into some rotting treasure chest. He did not know the ABC of Western logical thought. How was he to understand modern principles like communism? Sarwasvam had triumphantly asked how a fellow without any English could be a Revolutionary.

Birsa Munda felt that it was now his responsibility to save Mao's honour. But a colonial culture got in the way of a declaration that English had nothing to do with Revolution. The whoring after English stopped him short of such a statement. So he argued bullishly that not only did Mao know English, he was quite an expert at it. He gave examples to buttress his argument.

Mao knew very good English. White folk were often astonished by the fluency he displayed. Besides, he taught his comrades English grammar. That's why they called Mao mahaamahopaadhyaaya, Greatest Guru. Thus, Birsa Munda.

Oh! And which book do you cite for an authority, questioned Sarwasvam. *Chuu Chuu Chaa Chaa*, a Chinese book, said Birsa Munda, without batting an eyelid.

What is the title of the English translation? asked Sarwasvam.

Not translated into English at all, said Birsa Munda. Ah ha! So you know Chinese! chuckled Sarwasvam with derision. Certainly. Very well. I speak fluent Chinese, cackled Birsa Munda.

May you be castrated! Cunning Brahminical bastard! ... fumed Sarwasvam deep within.

Years ago.

5

Birsa Munda recalled Sarwasvam. Where was he? Personification of English, where was Sarwasvam now? Sarwasvam was a walking encyclopaedia. The English alphabits were his organs and limbs. Someone is said to have photographed Nature's shapes resembling ABCDs. Poor fellow wasted his effort. Could just as well have photographed Sarwaswam. Where, oh where, was this man?

Birsa Munda was almost deliriously repeating Sarwasvam's name. Had you, Sarwasvam, been around, Kanchinaadham would have been buried under the lava of quotations spewing forth. I, too, can quote a little from English. But if I cited from postmodern texts, I'd have little claim to Maoism. Declaring myself a champion Maoist has created acute limitations round me, regretted Birsa Munda. Had Sarwasvam been here at this hour, Kanchinaadham's brass-trumpet-tenor would have shattered under the onslaught of relentless English quotations, Sarwasvam's ultra-modern missiles. God! prayed Birsa Munda, send us Sarwasvam. Birsa Munda had, of course, forgotten that he was an unbeliever.

6

Sarwasvam came. The secret prayers of Birsa Munda bore fruit. Where have you been? Where were you all this while...asked all of them at once.

Without you, the Telugu world tasted like bland food without salt, said Pragatineni.

Without your quotations, life lacked zest, chipped in Birsa Munda. And, said Birsa Munda, even while we were discussing Maoism, Kanchinaadham turned up, like grit in sherbet...

Sarwasvam let fly a quotation. We cannot sleep with two mistresses at the same time, said prominent Italian philosopher Zeem Zaam. So we must concentrate upon our own. Must refer to European treatises for authenticity. Not take every country bumpkin seriously. He threw a disparaging glance at Kanchinaadham.

At all events, queried Birsa Munda, is Zeem Zaam a confirmed communist?

A Biocommunist, said Sarwasvam.

What's that? We've heard of bio-chemistry and bio-technology, said Pragatineni. But ... this?

The philosophic offspring of postmodern biology and postmodern communism, explained Sarwasvam.

Cloned ideas and cloned principles lead to socialism. This socialism is bio-communism. Socialist egalitarianism is impossible if each one thinks his way and for himself. Everyone must have the same thought, the same ideology. That is possible only through white chromosomes, Sarwasvam presented the distilled essence.

Which treatise proposes this theory? asked Birsa Munda.

Zeem Zaam's book *Reasoning and Free Motion* elaborates this theory – Sarwasvam cited the authority.

7

It was Bhagawantham's hospital. Bhagawantham was aghast seeing Sarwasvam return. He fell into deep thought trying to analyze this strange occurrence.

Your medicine missed the mark ... chemics turned contrary, said Sarwasvam stepping into the hospital. Accused him of gross negligence of life. Doctor Bhagawantham was dumb struck.

Doctorji, I wrote you the letter living in the lap of a remote village of Assam. I wrote that I was freed of my ailment, meaning freed of knowledge. That was a delusion. I wrote the letter in that state of hallucination.

But my illusions were short-lived. Suddenly I was gripped by fever. Body became sapless; lacked stamina. I lapsed into delirium and babble. I was assailed by a clutch of nightmares – white devils crushing me to pulp with heaps of weighty books. There was a famine of sleep. Friends took me to Dr. Malhotra in the town. He diagnosed it as a case of thoughtless abstinence and starvation. My body was shocked by the starvation and was declining into an irreversibly critical state. It was the hasty and unhealthy step I had taken – of abstinence from regular indulgence in English quotations.

Dr. Malhotra was a great psychiatrist. He had specialized in the area of neuro-linguistics. His research findings were that Indians did not have mother tongues. Mother tongues were dead. We are only translating from the English into our languages. Speaking naturally in mother tongues was a lost practice among educated gentry. Ours was now entirely a translated expression. That's how, token conversing in Telugu was, in reality, conversing in English; perfunctory writing in Telugu was in reality writing in English. Mother tongues died long, long ago, said Malhotra.

He did research on pet dogs to learn about language. He studied keenly the behavioural aspects of thousands of pet dogs. He toured all states to conduct his research. Pet dogs responded well and with ease to calls in English. They instantly obeyed commands in English. They are doing everything when ordered in English. Mother tongues do not have such commanding power.

English is not just a language; it is essential to life itself. Since long, English has become a life-sustaining basic need...like air and water. A mutation has occurred in us making English a part of our genetic code. This is Dr. Malhotra's scientific inference. His thesis asserts that English commands our brain and through its neurological processes the functioning of our organs.

After his thorough research on pet dogs, Dr. Malhotra turned his attention to a study of intellectuals. The inferences and results were no different. That man is also animal, and an intelligent animal at that, is established in this way, too, says Malhotra.

All right, let us put aside the issue of dogs for a moment. Let us chat, desultorily perhaps, about our intellectuals. They firmly believe that every idea is rendered authentic only through supporting English quotations. Were one to make one's own sentence without a supporting quotation, it wouldn't appear authentic to them but be like indistinct sounds, blown away by breezes. Such a speaker of independent sentences would, by the nature of his language, automatically be excluded from the class of intellectuals. The reason is that a great transformation has occurred in our brain. This is not visible to the naked eye, or observable to ignorant minds. This great change is something Dr.Malhotra observed very scientifically. It was a change of evolutionary significance.

It was thanks to this research that he became a world-renowned psychiatrist.

Dr. Malhotra told Sarwasvam – The change that swept over all intellectuals is precisely the change that has swept you away... *in extremis*. It is not that you resonate to the English language. It is that your universe itself is an English universe. No trace of any other, such as native.

If someone said to you in Telugu 'adugo puli', you'll not experience any fear. You will not shiver, you'll not sweat. Because you must first translate it in your mind into English. You'll have to translate the utterance into 'there tiger' and only then quiver suitably. The genetic system and reflex of your living body declines all acceptance of Telugu as Telugu. There is no way of your understanding any complex sentences in your mother tongue. Your body will not accept them. How you have won acclaim as a Telugu intellectual is a huge surprise to me.

But again, perhaps, it is not surprising, said Malhotra.

Yes, nothing surprising at all. Telugu died long ago. All that is alive now is English. Yet, English did not mother our tongue. So it is not easy to think deeply or express complex ideas through English. It is possible only to borrow from across the oceans. That's why you have morphed into a computer that furnishes quotations all the time. This is the thing that's made you an intellectual. The mutation that occurred in everyone has assumed radical proportions in you. This is what has brought you recognition as an intellectual. You better continue this activity.

Know well... be cautioned. Continue the task of gathering up quotations ... and then ... spewing them out without any stops. Else you'll contract a fearsome disease, Dyspepsia Intellectuallosa Anglicana. Intellectual indigestion is the prime source of all disorders.

Your sudden giving up of English quotations was wrong, terribly wrong. That brings danger to life itself. If an alcoholic suddenly stopped drinking, that would bring danger to life. This is exactly the same.

I returned to my old ways. Malhotra's advice was right.

Doctor Bhagawantham sighed an aside, "Bhagwan"!

Sarwasvam expressed his angst – This English knowledge and this import of English quotations is killing my creativity. On the other hand, if I gave it all up, I am sure to die. I want to live, Doctorji, I want to live – sobbed Sarwasvam.

Doctor Bhagawantham tried to console him. What can not be avoided must be loved. It is good to take to it as ones life, ones destiny.

Doctorji, what you are using is the tongue of personality development. Not mother tongue. We have killed our mother. Now there is no salvation, said Sarwasvam, as he walked away, dejected, head bowed.

8

Sarwasvam committed suicide. He went under a speeding missile of an electric train, and died an ultra-modern death. In a flash his form frayed into fragments. It is difficult to even imagine what that death must have been like.

Within moments.

Dust gathered in thick layers upon Telugu books, and Telugu won the status of an ancient language. Reason... the man who ushered Telugu into the modern world, Sarwasvam, had ceased.

Sarwasvam, more than any others, had recognized one truth. Telugu did not gain modernity naturally. It was an imported modernity, a brokered modernity; none of its own. Telugu language was dependent. So, one must give up all delusory pretence of original thought and original writing. This fact was known to all intellectuals, yet none had assimilated it as much as Sarwasvam had. That's why, so long as he lived, he never thought originally, never spoke originally.

Abjuring ones original thought is much more difficult than giving up ones property. That requires much wisdom. Sarwasvam had achieved such wisdom.

The thought that he was no more, terrified the intellectual class as much as if word went around town that all convent schools had shut down in the land of the Telugus. Because, many writers had benefited from Sarwasvam's existence, won awards. Whatever he said was supported by an English quotation. Thus their writing gained authenticity. So and so white writer said exactly the same thing, said Sarwasvam; and their work immediately rose a few notches above Telugu. Great honour.

During British rule, if a newborn was fair, people were thrilled – the infant was so like a white sahib! Similarly, when Sarwasvam cited a white author to compare a Telugu writer's work, they felt honoured, that their work had exceeded expectations of Telugu standards. The authors swelled with the joy that they, too, had become international. When Sarwasvam died, intellectuals wept copiously. After all, he was a selfless man who had dedicated his life to colonial thought and colonial tongue.

9

It was Shivaraatri. A Shivaraatri that was like a *Kaala Raatri*, dark night, a witness to the crack of doom, thought Kanchinaadham. It was the day Sarwasvam had killed himself. But Kanchinaadham did not regard the event a tragic one. He thought of it as *vimukti*, release. For Shivaraatri to turn vicious there is a strong reason. That's why that night spent itself in tortuous wakefulness.

Shiva was the cause of dissolution. Dissolution leaves a void, a horrific vacuum. Not even tears can subsist.

Kanchinaadham had grasped the meaning of dissolution when he saw an infant's corpse in his childhood. Mother's journey from silence into Silence... then, too, he had seen the mortal dance of the *Kapaaladhaari*, skull-bearer. The smile disappearing from the sister's face; the sister herself, mother's womb-sharer, disappearing tracelessly... vanishing from sight, dying, tortuous separations ... all these are Shiva's, the ultimate solvent's, different funereal, macabre ballets, deathly pantomimes of the sentinels at death's portals, the ghastly broad grins of Death's ushers.

But the vacuum of this Shivaraatri was more extensive; indeed, all-encompassing, taking all into its fold. It was the true face of death, no mere mask.

Saroja ran into him in the Mukkaamala Shivaalayam street. They stood under the peepul tree.

I am pregnant, said Saroja.

Kanchinaadham smiled and said, Joyous news, whoever be the cause.

It is a female foetus in my womb, she said.

Greater joy! Goddess Lakshmi... or Parvati Devi.

How that infant looks, how it will be... we'll never see, said Saroja failing to staunch the flow of tears. That infant will permanently dissolve into Shiva, without our ever seeing her. Her voice choked with *dukkha*.

She recounted. Upon examination, doctor confirmed that that it was a female child. Conducted modern tests on the foetus and determined sex in the zygotic stage itself. Husband has strongly favoured aborting. The husband, Lord-Master, was sure that only a male child could redeem the generations, and the family. Girl-child was a burden on earth, he was cocksure.

For having a son who could sustain the family, one had to perform a holy ritual, *Pumsavanam*, according to the *Dharmasuutra*. This rite had to be performed while the woman was pregnant.

Kanchinaadham had heard a great deal about such rites from his father, Deekshitulu. Such rites had been laid down and described in the *Apasthambha Gruhyasuutra*. The rites were a belief. No verfiable results existed.

But modern medicine's sex determination tests were playing an efficient role in the extinction of the class – woman. More effectively than the beliefs of the *Dharmasuutra*. There was no drum-beating, crowd of people, forcible thrusting into the funeral pyre, raking the flames and splinters of wood – none of that ghastly mess.

Killing infants with a grain of rice in their mouth and other such rustic practices were now totally unnecessary. It would all be accomplished neatly in the aseptic environs of hospital buildings, where silence reigned.

Crores of foetuses would disappear from the womb itself. No evidence of the brutal killings. A world of silence.

Innumerable killings of the foetal kind occurred in a modern Hindu colonial state named Gujarat. Now, this modern violence had entered a traditional home in Mukkaamala.

The childhood memory of the infant corpse flushed in the canal came flooding. People had crowded around. A common sigh went up, like that unfortunate infant. What a pitiless mother, cursed some. Others remarked that she may have severed the umbilical connection in some truly helpless state.

Such tell-tale signs are not found now. High modern technology has ushered in silent violence, nano-violence. The dead aren't seen; the murderers aren't seen. The whole universe is under a pall of horrific, silent dissolution. Perhaps this is what's called the cloud of doom, *pralaya megha*.

10

Running away from that *pralaya megha,* Kanchinaadham slipped into a lonely sleep in his solitary room. He'd popped a sleeping pill, and went into a deep sleep.

A curious dream. A frightening great luminiscence had enveloped Mukkaamala. It was a great floodlight. It was such an extreme, sharp luminiscence that the brightness at the Pragatineni marriage pandal dimmed in memory. There was no stopping it. It penetrated deep into the crevices of the bridge. The Mukkaamala canal glowed blinding-bright, with the flames of the burnished light.

Massive shields also could not repulse that brightness. Then what chance human bodies?

The light rays tore through skin and penetrated the bodies. Everything was transparent. Before him stood Saroja.

Kanchinaadham screamed, a sharp piercing cry.

Your womb is empty, the shelter of foetus...

Then, recovering, asked, What is the source of this whitening darkness, darkling brilliance? How did this lightning explosion occur?

Look up, she said. An artificial sun glowered. Kanchinaadham woke up in a sweat. Recalled his father's words...this world is dream-like.

11

It is colonial modernism that brought us from sleep into wakefulness, and from dreams to reality, said Hanumantha Rao, alias Birsa Munda.

This is Pragatineni's magnificient mansion. Glowing with expensive brilliance. Kanchinaadham is narrowing his eyelids with some unease. His eyes are not yet accustomed to so much brightness.

Birsa Munda is lecturing – English language built a huge bridge. It united the people of the Indian continent, indeed united the Bharatakhanda with the universe. A universal humanism took incarnation. Human relations got strengthened.

Pragatineni chipped in with a curious statement – Not just human relations, animal relations also got strengthened. He began citing the world-renowned psychiatrist Dr. Malhotra's opinions in support.What Dr.Malhotra asserted was – Whether in Hyderabad, Delhi or in New York, dogs respond alike to the English language. Addressed by English names, they promptly run up to you and begin wagging tails. Obey English commands instantly.

That is the power of the English language. English is the language of the workers; English is human language, animal language, divine language. It is everything, said Pragatineni.

He declared the Telugu language dead. Everyone was taken aback by Pragatineni's declaration. Reminded him of his great and selfless service to Telugu. Mentioned the Telugu literature he published and popularized. It wasn't appropriate that he should single-handedly have accomplished this much for Telugu, only to coolly announce its death, to betray it in deepest consequence. They said that Pragatineni's healthy and prosperous life was proof of Telugu's good health and longevity. He was Telugu personified. His tongue was the eternal Telugu edict.

Pragatineni curled his lips in disapproval. What we call Telugu books are not Telugu books at all. They are English Books masquerading as Telugu ones. Actually the language of Guntur and Krishna districts is a colonial creation. This is the language that rules imperiously over journals, books and cinema. It is posturing as the standard language of cultural refinement. Where is the colloquial, dialectal Telugu? It has vanished out of sight. Is there any Telugu in the accents of television anchors? Indeed, is there any remote substance in it?... asked Pragatineni.

His words surprised, even dazed, everyone. Is he poking himself in the eye? What's this self-destruct mode? He is himself a man from the Krishna district. What, then, is the reason for this sudden, quirky change?

In response to Pragatineni, one writer proclaimed proudly that he, among some others, wrote in regional varieties of Telugu.

These are artificial responses, said Pragatineni, irritably. Then he gave vent to his sorrow in a serious and sad tone.

Bosom friend Sarwasvam's death has made me sleepless. What is the meaning implicit in his death? I saw that horrific death with wide, unbelieving eyes. All his shattered body lay scattered like an unstrung garland of the English alphabet. A few, sad, last quotations thrust out of the mangled brain. Pages of a new English paperback spattered with blood fluttered a little in the wind. I stared in dismay, wondering whether it was Sarwasvam or some European tourist. Assuredly it was

Sarwasvam's cadaver. That death was Sarwasvam's. Promptly, without the slightest delay, all of you wrote elegies. What temerity...what hearts!! Why don't you write elegies for yourselves! Do you believe you're all alive? Growled Pragatineni, glowering at them all.

Birsa Munda remarked that Pragatineni was probably drunk. It was, of course, true; when he spoke, the strong smell shook them. This was the first time such a thing happened. Pragatineni is a highly disciplined man. Each part of his body appears composed compactly, rationally. His attire is also similarly composed. There is great consistency in him. His is a new-age automobile body set according to rigorous mathematical principles. His movements are unhesitant and healthily pure. He looks like the chief manager of a multinational company. He also appears to have the power to confer a multinational status on literature. Emaciated, gaunt poverty also turns into a beautiful model in his presence.

Was it the same Pragtineni who spoke!... wondered everyone.

Yes I am drunk. Dead drunk; agreed Pragatineni. I have awakened my inner consciousness in this way to resurrect the real Sarwasvam buried inside me. I have awakened him in this drunken stupor.

Then he fell to attacking writers and intellectuals. You have written elegies for Sarwasvam; are you all, all alive? I saw an English movie. One gentleman is shown controlling a whole colony through a remote-control. He turns a high-traffic, chaotic bazaar into a static, orderly still-life through the remote control. Ours is a remote-control language, remote-control literature, remote-control life. That's why we went down on our knees before the white-man and licked his boots asking – give us freedom, give us equality, annihilate caste, give us language, give us thought, give us life, give us food, give us water, give us oxygen, give us coca-cola, give us jobs in cola-companies, give us garbage, give us wastes, give us scrap, give us atoms, give us atom bombs, give us enemies, give us friends, give us religion, give us nationality, give us a flag, give us festivals, give us condoms... for such dependents as us, how shall there be independent stories? Yours are dollar–tales that go around robed as rupaiah-tales; dhoti-clad dollar-stories of the paraiah kind... Pragatineni boomed.

Madya, wine, is one of the sacred *pancha-makaaraas* – *Madya*, *Maamsa*, *Matsya*, *Mudra*, and *Maithuna* – according to the ancient *vaamaachaaryas.* An Imbibing of that sacred libation inspired Pragatineni with the spirit of Amba, Divine Mother, and made him voice Truth.

This is not our life, said Pragatineni. There is nothing to write about it. Earth has become an alien planet... he sighed.

There is much to write about, especially about dalits, said Suvarnam.

Pragatineni fell to ranting at this. This fellow is a dalit writer; he dishes out garbled, rhetorical, unmeaning trash. He displays false humility, bends and bows and scrapes around for awards. Why doesn't someone write an elegy for him, asked Pragatineni in sheer excitement. Suvarnam rose and gave him a resounding slap.

Suvarnam was a dalit writer. A dalit writer who had won tremendous popular acclaim. His style was entirely consistent with traditional rhetoric. He was capable of turning tempestuous anger into a storm in teacup. Could transform growling tigers into meeoowing kittens. An uncanny ability to transmogrify, that won him awards and honours; not one award that escaped him, not one honour that evaded him. Not one who opposed him lived on this earth. Suvarnam was *ajaatashatru*, had no foes. He was a dalit Manmatha, the lord of amours who could change armouries into flower-arcades, barbs into boquets, win hearts with the ease of his appeasing admonishments.

Prominent critic Sarwasvam had written voluminous criticism on Suvarnam's writings. Lavished praise on him for exemplary postmodernist work. He quoted profusely from Suvarnam's writings to demonstrate that seminal ideas of Western thinkers such as Zeem Zaam, Bo Gus Muun, Duum Damm, Neil Knaile irrigated Telugu literary fields dripping through Suvarnam's works. He valued Suvarnam's work as the golden jewellery of Telugu *kaavyakanya*, poetic muse. Suvarnam was esteemed a great writer capable of yoking the London Museum with the thickets of Africa. He was a Telugu writer only for namesake. Actually his work was western effluence, purged and untouched by human hand. In fact Sarvaswam's entire critical eminence arose from his exegesis of Suvarnam's work.

Suvarnam was a die-hard disciple and follower of Pragatineni who promoted Suvarnam a great deal. And Pragtineni had his comeuppance from Suvarnam! Exchange of words grew so much that slamming turned to slapping; Suvarnam gave Pragatineni a tight one. Pragatineni could not take the insult. His eyes welled up with tears. Intense agitation wracked his body.

This base ingratitude, he said, is the rght honour I deserve. All this time I have lain dead under the weight of your garlands and shawls. For your sake, your writings' sake, for your fame's sake, I sucked every bastard who offered in return anything at all. He continued...

But you... sobbed an excited Pragatineni... you blabbering buffoons have never shut up. For you have I fallen! Fallen so low! So long I fell! For you... and Pragatineni broke down.

Suvarnam came down harshly. You are a merchant; you sell literature.

True. You spoke true. I agree I am a purveyor of literature. By nature I am businessman. Business is in my blood. Business is ingrained in our rationalist, progressivist communism.

Rationalism and Progressivism freed us from the bonds of rural life. They awakened the trading instincts in us. That's the secret of our caste and its success. We are proud exporters of colonialism all over the globe; we are the original expansionists. We gave Imperialism its wide canvas.

We are the heroes, we are art, we are literature, we are fashion technology, we are the computer, we are trade, we are revolution, we are commercial revolution, we are revolutionary commerce. We are the real force that advance your stories; it is our pens that script them, it is our caste that cast them in the mould of success – thus spoke Pragatineni, in his cosmic form. It was the *vishwaruupa* of postmodern progressivism.

They gaped in awe at this infinitely diaphanous business body, a *shuukshma sareera* that wrapt the earth entirely. And they prostrated at his feet.

Oh Great Soul! O Solar Luminosity! Bless us with a narration of your divine life-story, they pleaded.

Pragatineni began narrating the story of his incarnation.

My progenitor was a great Rationalist. He harboured no belief in God. He reposed his belief entirely in wealth. He supplanted the all-existing God with the axiom that wealth was the root of the world (*dhana moolam idam jagat*). First he transformed agriculture into trade. He was not just a trader, though; he was a revolutionary, too. A man who boldly strode from green revolution into blue revolution … my Father. Later he came to Vijayawada and translated literature into trade, books into business. Shaped schools into shops, changed collegiate education into corporate commerce. He turned wind and water into warehousing opportunities. Was there anything beyond the scope of trade? Rayalaseema revolution's bullets were turned into factionist firearms by our revolutionary brother, comrade Suuryudu. Truly, businessmen were very good fellows, said Pragatineni in an aside. He asserted with conviction that businessmen were more honest than our progressive intellectuals. His assertions boomed like drum-beats. And now he carried on in this vein, without further reference to the Father (good fathers pass on their businesses to sons, and wither away like the State).

I assert, said Pragatineni, that traders are good people because at least occasionally their conscience shakes free of the inebriating success of business. That's why big businessman Bajaj broke loose with invective on Bill Gates. Fuelled by a nationalist spirit, a swadeshi India-made spirit, he launched a broadside at Bill Gates. You are looter, yours is not philanthropy, said Bajaj; it's not love but leeching. It was a washing down that Bajaj gave with an awakened conscience – a chastisement with the valour of tongue,[11] rare, hence precious.

But observe revolutionaries. What opportunism! No guts for truth. They write secret letters and journals about the commercialization of their comrades, the goondaism, the unslaked thirst for wealth. If these surface, they bite their tongues for foolishly committing themselves to words they can not recall. Then engage in convenient self-critique. But they do not dare publicly erase the boundaries between platitude and pelf. As for people…they are dumb and devilish at once. For an extra rupee's interest they'll believe any kind of bank or finance company. They'll worship an assassin or rapist if it suits their need. This little secret has been known to writers and singers. That's why they make deception their business...self-deception.

Hanumantha Rao alias Birsa Munda was enraged. You are drunk. There is no consistency, no logic, no causal equation in a drunkard's talk. So one need not mind drunken blather; their talk is autocratic... not substantial, he fumed.

Drunken talk rises from the subconscious. That talk is real truth, opined Ajooba.

You speak the language of Freudism. Communists don't accept that, countered Birsa Munda.

Dalits don't accept it, either, said Suvarnam.

Telangana-proponents don't accept it either, piped in a Telangana-voice.

12

Pragatineni collapsed in a heap. Pain skewered through his heart. Meeting such resistance for the first time... that was the cause. He had been recognized as a distinguished gentleman. His reputation took a beating for the first time. He could not tolerate the onslaught.

The poised gentleman Pragatineni disappeared temporarily. In his place emerged a totally contrary form that had lain dormant.

Everything transforms into its opposite. Pragatineni was now an emblem of this Truth. The submerged contrary form now became manifest. A totally illogical, unusual form shook its mane, awakening from its deep slumber. The second coming of Pragatineni struck terror in the hearts of his intellectual friends. This was the beast. Everyone agreed that this demonaic form must be annihilated.

The obvious reason for this unusual manifestation was the libation of liquor. Ancients believed that intoxicants had supernatural powers. In the Vedic age, Aryans routinely indulged in liquor, *soma paana*. Rural folk routinely drink fresh toddy at village Fairs. Vaamaachaarins, a cult who deeply believed in unorthodox ritual practices, esteemed liquor as a holy drink.

The reason? Intoxication compels the emergence of our inner self, a self which we do not approve. Liquour lets loose our inner self, manifests the Truth that lies suppressed by our routine, well-disciplined alertness.

This is what happened to Pragatineni.

Sarwasvam's death deeply agitated him. He drowned his sorrow in drink. As a result a hidden face of Pragatineni surfaced. It met with instant rejection. That rejection brought on the heart-attack.

13

Pragatineni was admitted into a huge corporate hospital. He slipped into a comatose state. He was being given artificial respiration. He was close to death.

At such a time the clatter of boots broke the silence. A gentleman came to the bedside. Whispered something in Pragatineni's ears. Then traced his steps back.

Promptly Pragatineni's respiration became normal. Heart beat was restored to statistical precision. He recovered. Death disappered from the threshold.

What reason? What did the stranger whisper in the ear? Some magical, miraculous chant? Indeed, who was that stranger?

Doctors were astonished. How did the stranger accomplish what they could not despite expensive training abroad? What was the great power hidden in that stranger? How did his Word acquire such powers? Indeed, who was he?

Let it be known then ... what he'd uttered in the ear was no magic mantra. Amazingly, it was immensely more powerful, though. 'Our Government is formed'. That was the utterance.

Elections had been held recently. Election results were declared. Pragatineni's caste had raised the victory pennant. Their community flag flew high. The stranger was no stranger to Pragatineni. He was a partner in the liquor business.

The scenario had changed. The strong whiff of bubbling malt all over, business over-brewing, suppressed the conscience that had just recently created such a nuisance, the cause of all trouble. Pragatineni's brief convalescence restored to him his gentleman's status.

Intellectuals and writers, businessmen, collected and crowded round him. A distinguished gentleman, Pragatineni announced good tidings with a dignified smile lighting his face. Soon I am about to publish a compilation of stories. That volume will be launched in California. On that occasion, we propose to honour the dalit writer Suvarnam, who glitters like the golden tiara of dalit literature.

Suvarnam touched Pragatineni's feet. In genuflection. A round of clapping thundered.

14

Kanchinaadham was acutely agitated by Saroja's decision to terminate her pregnancy...was tragically saddened by her resolve to pluck out his surrogate form from within... after all, it was Saroja who had given him relief, redeemed him from his uncreativity! Salvation was nipped in the bud as foetus was being aborted. Nirvaana was transformed into mere *niryaana*, death. A mere beginning was turned to a definite ending. Kanchinaadham remained cursed to an uncreative life. Like his's ideas, this conception too just disappeared into oblivion.

Geos had turned into cosmos. Rooted earth had formed into formless space. That's why bhoogola turned boring. As Kanchinaadham muttered aloud, pedestrians flashed alien looks.

The Earth was a vagrant in vacuous space. Escaping the atmosphere into outer space like a cosmonaut, no force that could anchor, no pulsating force riding its rhythms, the earth rolled on, all gravity lost, an unmeaning manifestation. It transformed to space... that is it. Everything turns into its other, thought Kanchinaadham.

Kanchinaadham went to Peddapuram Maridamma-temple street. Sundari's house was on that street. It had been long since he'd visited that house. So he went hesitantly looking for landmarks. No sign of Sundari inside. Some other girl winked an invitation. That was not Sundari! What happened to her?

Kanchinaadham's heart beat fearfully. A customer, or perhaps pimp, stood there smoking. Kanchinaadham asked him about Sundari. Sundari? Who's that?

Kanchinaadham walked the lanes and bylanes asking for Sundari's whereabouts.

No one told him. One pimp replied, rather peevishly. Many girls come here and go from here. No one even remembers their names. Buying and selling goes on. Girls from here are sent to Mumbai, too. And girls bought in Mumbai are brought here. This is big business. Don't ask names. Don't ask addresses. Fresh stocks come in daily; better and better stock. By the way, how much cash in your pocket?

Kanchinaadham's heart was occupied by a vacancy. Now, more than ever before, were people getting sold. Sundari whirled in his heart. She was whore. That which gets sold by the second is whore; that which gets picked by the pinch is whore; that which gets consigned to commerce is whore. How can she be located or sighted? Peddapuram or Mumbai? What could be her language? That which gives up language is whore.

Inexplicable grief clutched Kanchinaadham's heart at every loss. Lost language, lost emotion, lost infant, lost woman… each loss caused deep anguish in him...KK...

Felt as if living in sad times, when everything was eroding, dissolving and losing its identity. Felt as if an immense vacancy, a measureless vacuum engulfed the universe.

A clay-doll, of uncertain vintage, uncannily reappeared at home. The pretty doll had been made by elder sister. She'd even painted it. Now the colours had faded; the nose had fallen off. Its form was steadily disintegrating. Tears welled in Kanchinaadham's eyes.

The colours, complexions, hues and glows in sister's face were slowly dissipating.

The sparkle of life in her eyes had dimmed.

The zest of youthfulness died in her youth.

All the tragic turns in akkayya's life moved about hazily in his heart. Where is she now? Is she alive at all? What happened? Should she appear again ... What if she appeared again? What use? Can he see the akkayya of the past? Can he see the zest and the spirit of the past?

Can not bring back akkayya's glorious face from the past....can not turn time back like one turned back scenes, songs and reels at the Mukkaamala Touring Talkies...

15

Vanishing language, vanished thought, vanished infant, vanished woman – troubled Kanchinaadham.

Most of all, the disappearance of languages hurt him most. Death of people did not matter much. Death of a language is certain death of a civilization. Annihilating a language is real genocide. This terrible massacre has been going on at will in the cosmos.

The very first time for man, Yuri Gagarin, a Russian citizen, defied earth's attraction and set foot in the cosmos. That transformed the very form of the *bhoomandala.*

Everyone acclaimed Yuri Gagarin, the first to open the doors to cosmos, as the Columbus of the Cosmos. Columbus had found the continents, had found the paths to push through to the continents. Gagarin overpowered gravity and forced open channels into the chaos of the cosmos.

What was the result?

We know the terrible consequences which resulted.

Columbus found the continents. Christian colonists coursed through to the centres of these continents and decimated countless communities, languages and cultures. Proclaimed theirs alone as civilization.

After Gagarin's cosmic foray, America contemplated a trip to the moon. Those were the days of American invasion of the Vietnam. Blood flowed in torrents. Thousands of American troops perished in the Vietnam war. Criticism within America was reaching a fever-pitch. People all over the world condemned the pitched-war as a vicious act. Imperial America planned a moon-landing as a cover up action, to divert attention from the atrocity of MyLai. Black Americans and progressive intellectuals were quick to criticize this moon-trip as a conspiracy to divert the world's focused gaze from this destructive war.

America planted its flag on moon-land to shroud the war in forgetfulness. The flesh and blood offered at the altar of imperial ambition on earth was consigned to the shroud of a moon-shadow drawn across the cosmos. Thus the cosmos turned into an arena where imperial torture was carried out.

With this inauguration of a cosmic theatre, white imperialists began staging aggressions on world languages. Space provided routes to invade languages, wave after wave. Artificial satellites mounted waves of invasion on mother tongues and proceeded to murder them brutally. They also dealt extinction on local cultures.Language and culture had... now...only imperial colours.

Sarwasvam saw in this the advent of one world language. He praised this as a welcome development.

Kanchinaadham, however, was deeply depressed by this. He was now subject to fears that any language worth owning as ours was getting extinct.This sense of gloom continues in Kanchinaadham.

The world has shrunk into a little shanty town.

The world is expanding, the late Sarwasvam had felt. Kanchinaadham was strongly inclined to condemning Sarwasvam's belief. Expansion, said Kanchinaadham, means dilution of density, a state of collapsing into itself, shrinking. Everything transforms itself into its contradiction, he believed.

An unending debate raged between Kanchinaadham and Sarwasvam, as long as Sarwasvam lived.

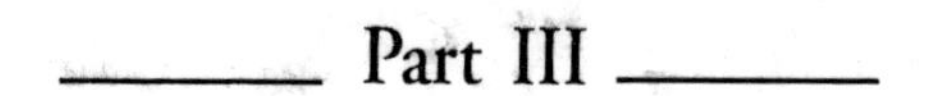

Part III

UGK

Communication
is impossible between human beings.

1

Koham. Who am I?

Sitting on the banks of the Mukkaamala canal, pelting pebbles, Kanchinaadham called himself into question – Who am I? Actually, is there a definite face to man? Is there a stable, changeless essence buried deep inside man? Meaning, does Aatman exist? The Buddha says that the world is Anaatman, without soul.

All right Aatman will be what it will. But yesterday's face does not exist today. Modern medical practice has made facial plastic surgery easy. What emotions does a man with a new face feel standing before a looking glass? What does he feel watching a plastered face? After all, it is a mirror image that gives man his individual personality! With that image erased, and confronted with a totally strange new form, what might be that person's experience? What mighty transformation?

Indeed, does recognition of ones form occur in the world of birds and beasts? Or is self-recognition a formal human feature?. The whole world is said to be a system of forms and names. *Vedandantins* assert that name and form are impermanent, temporary and playful, hence not true.

In such a fluxful world, in a rapid flow of name and form, what constitutes me? Again, why should such a query arise, queried Kanchinaadham. Sometimes he can not place himself; he can not even recall his face properly. Why he is here, he can not fathom. Does not understand why he lives at all, and what the purpose is. However far one went, however fast one went. Everything is Nothing.

This incompleteness holds all humanity in its grip. The deep chasm, the void, can not be filled in any way; impossible. The more doors he opens, the more the world expands, endless, desert-like. There is no end, no bank to it. No difference between going from Mukkaamala to Ambaajipet, and going from earth to another planet. It is one and the same. The world is endless. However far one went, however fast, there is no difference between walk and sleep. Flux and stasis are the same.

Watching distant stars in space, Kanchinaadham wondered – are there living beings up there among the celestial bodies? Is there a chance that man-like beings exist among them? One day, perhaps, such a discovery will be made. Just as people across continents were found, so will people across the cosmos be found. They may become companions to man.

Yet man will stand alone in the universe and continue to ask – Who am I? That question will cut like the rough teeth of a saw.

Man is bowed down by weighty knowledge, the more he excavates the world. The accumulated knowledge, of course, does not present any answers to the question – Who am I? Surely, there is no answer! Science makes an effort to answer questions about how the universe was formed and how it has been evolving. But the questions, why and wherefore, do not fall in its ambit. The vast knowledge that science has created is just that – knowledge. Questions of existence do not fit into the scope of knowledge. That is why the question – Who am I ? – stands alone. It exists in the very existence of man.

In a Russian science-fiction novel, a cosmonaut travels to a planet circling a far-off star. He falls in love with a woman there, but returns alone to earth, inevitably. Her call, however, keeps reaching the earth as a continuous signal. The cosmonaut drowns deep into grief.

Truly, on earth itself the distances between people appear vast and unbridgeable. Unclear signals, like strange interplanetary, intergalactic signals, pass between them. The signals do not bring people close together, do not close the gaps, do not fill vacuums. No ones existence can fill and complete another's scooped-out existence.

That is why the question – Who am I? – stands alone, eternally.

Man is not a loner. Society gives an answer to the question – Who am I – says Birsa Munda. Says he: historical transformations provide the answer.

Exactly! – says Pragatineni – historical change does.

Ajooba came huffing and puffing to a lazily contemplative Kanchinaadham, who was still asking himself who he was... He carried a message – Birsa Munda was possessed by an evil spirit.

2

Hanumantha rao, alias Birsa Munda, is trapped by an evil spirit, said Ajooba.

Really? – asked Kanchinaadham, quizzically.

Is that a metaphorical statement? He wondered. Europe was entrapped by an evil spirit called Communism, said Kanchinaadham, to elaborate his point. That kind?

No, a real evil spirit has taken possession of him. He even behaves like a possessed man, explained Ajooba.

Pishaacha Shaastra, the Book of Spirits, states clearly that people who die pining after desires, turn into *pishaachas* – poltergeists, ghosts and ghouls about town. As a child he had heard that if a pregnant woman died before completing the term, her corporeal aatman, *pretha,* turned into a ghost and wandered about, moaning. Similarly a suicide immediately turned into a presence, past turned inside-out, and restlessly groped about the dark.

There is only one great *maantrika,* exorcist who can free men from terrifying ghouls, and rid ghosts of nasty humans. Thopella Sankaram is his name.

Kanchinaadham went to Thopella Sankaram's house in the Visweswara *agrahaaram* and knocked at the doors. Those almost ancient doors opened, creaking, groaning like unsatisfied desires.

Thopella Sankaram thundered – Who are you, that, ghost-like, disturbs my summer noon's siesta?

I am a denizen of Mukkaamala village. I am of the Bharadwajasa gothra; my name is Kanchinaadham.

Don't irritate me; just tell me the purpose of your visit, said Sankaram.

Kanchinaadham launched into an ode on Sankaram's deep knowledge of the *Pishaacha Shaastra*, Demonology. Then he placed his query before Sankaram: Can ghosts possess non-believers?

Closing his eyes for a moment, Thopella Sankaram said, even communists can not escape the effects of karma, my boy! Don't non-believers have souls, hearts and desires? Everyone who dies grieving unsatisfied desires will surely turn into a ghost. This is truly Aanjaneya swaami's own teaching in the *Pishaacha Tantra*.

You may not believe in ghosts, yet you may turn into a ghost. All is destiny, the moving finger's writ in the folds of your forehead, sighed Sankaram. Even communists can not escape karma, stressed Sankaram, again. If destined to election by Goddess Lakshmi, even communists who decry the right to property turn Propertied men. They prosper in their business, business thrives in them. They are translated into their contradictions. Karma transforms; dissolute karma transforms damned absolutely.

Likewise, cautioned Sankaram gaaru, when in line for ghost-hood, by destiny driven to a devilish state, no one can escape the grief and pain of ghost-hood.

He proceeded, rather crestfallen – Pishaachaas of our time and Pishaachaas of present times are different. They, too, are transformed into a new generation-kind, with the passage of time.

Then Sankaram went on to opening an ancient trunk and picking up palm-leaf texts from it. They were very old and very brittle. Priceless, ancient texts, sighed Sankaram. Kanchinaadham sensed that the magical vigour of a great scholar of the Evil Books was on the wane in Sankaram. No more necromancy for him. No more magical ravishment.

He was a centurion. Almost skeletal to look at, thin skin glued over. No knowing what ghostly power sustained his life. This ghostly knowledge was useless, said Sankaram. These old Books of Evil do not suffice to grasp newer poltergeists. With changing times, the forms and substances of these ghosts are changing, too. They have grown beyond our intelligence. That's why this old scholarship is of no avail. The power of the mantra is failing.

Yet, these ghosts are surely better than humans. Ghosts believe in men, see!Men no longer acknowledge the Pishaacha! There is no greater superstition than the belief that ghosts don't exist, said Thopella Sankaram with utter, wondrous conviction. My own children are deeply mired in superstition. They disavow ghosts. They say it is just delusion.

But then, isn't the world itself an illusion! Like the serpent and the rope? How justified is it to discredit ghosts alone as delusion? A vedantic view treats men and the world itself as illusions. It is unfair to dismiss ghosts alone as illusions. What should one call faithless children of a great necromantic scholar such as I? So stubbornly dismissive of ghosts and spirits as illusions! Haven't I seen so many pishaachaas with these, mine own eyes! I have bound and controlled, commanded so many pishaachaas. *Haam-phut*, said I, and arrested and restrained ghouls and ghosts with the great *maantric* and *taantric* powers at my disposal. Lived as ghost among ghosts. Slept fearlessly in the midst of the *pramathagana*, ranged varieties of demons. Became the *Hanumathswapna*, the nightmarish vision of their nemesis, Lord Hanumaan. That the very sons of such a demonologist, a powerhouse of mantra endowed with powers without count, should decry pishaacha as superstition, speak frivolously, time and again... a normally composed Thopella Sankaram choked tearfully.

Watch, he said, and took off the towel covering his torso. His body was marked with scars, a testimony to the cruelty of ghosts.

Sankaram gaaruu, I am of the firm conviction that you are an avatar, an exorcist born for the good of the world. One of my friends is possessed by a ghost. I came, said Kanchinaadham, to apprise you of this event.

Thopella Sankaram told Kanchinaadham to bring his friend to the village burial ground at midnight on an *amaavaasya* day.

3

Birsa Munda was possessed by the spirit of Sarwaswam, none other. Kanchinaadham grasped this fact in a moment. The gestures and expressions, the idiom and style of speech, all pointed to Sarwasvam. Only the shape was Birsa Munda. *Mores,* and *Corpus*. *Anima* and *Persona*. Sarwasvam and Munda. *Aatma* and *Shareera*.

Why did you choose Birsa Munda, asked Kanchinaadham.

We are soul-brothers, Munda and I, ghoulish Sarwasvam said spiritedly. He enumerated and explained the bases of this fraternity – The two of us earned much knowledge at universities. Preferred knowledge to experience. Stepped out of narrow parishes into the sweep of urbanity. We are cognates.

No, retorted Kanchinaadham. There is no comparison. You torture him needlessly. Let go of him, he thundered.

Eyes blood-shot, the ghoul in Munda insisted they were from the same gothra, shared the same ancient womb.

Don't burn and blaze our blood-bond. Don't set us asunder, Munda said, pouncing on Kanchinaadham, going for his throat.

The bellowing shrieks shook the walls as Munda shook Kanchinaadham by the throat. But Kanchinaadham was unfazed.

Boldly he displayed amulet on his arm and said you can not terrify me… I have the amulet Thopella Sankaram gave.

With that, the terrified ghost collapsed all in a heap.

Then Kanchinaadham brought to the fore the distinction between Munda and Sarwasvam. There is much difference between you and Munda. Munda is a Maoist. The rural is his life. Mao closed down all universities. Made intellectuals march to villages. Taught them to learn from rural folk. That is Munda's way. Yours is different.

Promptly Sarwasvam retorted – Nonsense, there is no Maoism in India. Only Marxism. Pure, imported European Marxism. Our pioneers, ancestors took birth from Western Colonialism. What did Mao know? Did he have a doctorate? I respect Marx; he did a Ph.D from a university. That too, a European university. Research at a European university, mind you! Mao, on the other hand, was a village bumpkin with no regular school certificate even, retorted Sarwasvam.

What great things did a Ph.D do for you ? Turned you into a ghost! Kanchinaadham rebuked.

Sarwaswam said, Scholarly Ghosts are the best ghosts. They are respected all over the world.

He scoffed at Kanchinaadham for being a low-grade Brahmin who could not have known this. Truly, a man without modern education, one who has never seen the facade of a modern university, can never even begin to understand people. To analyze and understand people, one must know modern methodology. Such methodology is available only in the universities, that, too, chiefly in European universities in plentifuls.

Continued Sarwasvam: Such power is not available to the Orient nor to oriental texts. Understanding oriental texts also entails an inevitable resort to Western analytical tools. That methodology is the sole refuge, reiterated Sarwasvam. Birsa Munda knows this fully well; he is not a rural moron like Mao, asserted the semi-corporeal soul. Birsa Munda is the modern man who enabled the transmigration of colonialism and imperialism into Mao's corporeal frame, said Sarwasvam, investing the deed with great honour.

Why do you say so? Birsa Munda has publicized the notion that he is a Maoist.

Does one become something by merely claiming to be so? Indeed, asked Sarwasvam aggressively, is Birsa Munda really himself?

Birsa Munda is a Brahmin. A completely urbanized Brahmin. He changed his name to project himself as the peer of a great tribal warrior. That is to say, he wore the mantle of a tribal warrior – Birsa Munda – as a camouflage for his real existence as the Brahminical Hanumantha Rao. Does that ruse make him a tribal hero? Does change of name transform an individual? This question lurked under the lingering ghost's presence.

That's all right, Sarwasvam. Why did you seek asylum in Munda's body? Why have you become a parasite? Were you pained by the sudden disembodiment? Pining for incorporation, did you just choose as alternative the first body you found – Birsa Munda's – at random, asked he.

Or, is there some meaning hidden from us, O' great phantom?

Is Birsa Munda your proxy-form? What is the moan that burrows the earthen body of Birsa Munda? O' omniscient fantasm, pray you! Untie the secret knot of this mystery, and make me wise, pleaded Kanchinaadham.

The Evolution of Ghosts

Pishaacha Sarwasvam said softly: Lack of body bothers me not at all. I was released from bondage to body while being quite alive, claimed he, curiously. The ties to suffocating surroundings were unseamed when life still surged through the body. Body was no longer a need. Body turned burden. Indeed body stopped making sense. Body transformed into bodilessness. Manifest body turned unmanifest. Stimulus – Response, relationships ceased altogether for me. So the body appeared vain, a vestige to get rid of in the process of evolution. This caused my transmutation into a ghost. PishaachaSarwasvam gave a perfectly scientific explanation for his condition.

But Kanchinaadham was needled by scientific doubts. Magnificient genius!, enlighten me – Is your transformation into ghosthood empirically material or abstractly qualitative? Did you change day by day, stage by stage, progressively? Or did you change spontaneously, sublimating like boiling water into vapours, asked Kanchinaadham trying hard to illuminate his question. Quantitative, or qualitative... you know...

Quantitative change leads to qualitative change. Quantity determines quality; they are inversely proportional – the rarer the material, the greater the quality and potency. This is Revolutionary change, said PishaachaSarwasvam in a stern tone. It is the same as evolution. Evolutionary change induces phenomenal change. Many Western intellectuals have taught that all evolution in universe passes through these two stages. I have forgotten the names of these men in the hurry to transform into this magnificent spiritual state. With my fantastical powers, however, I can recall those names, but it will take some time. I am mutated into a Pishaacha only as the consequence of this formula of change, i.e., through the evolutionary and phenomenal stages. Now, I have gone beyond these two stages to become rarity itself, a Pishaacha, surpassed them and only then turned into this insubstantial, phantasmic stage. I have now stepped into the world of these ghosts, a brave new world.

O' immortally secure, infinitely intelligent ghost who have made the resort of Rudra, the site of Shiva, your abode! Explain to my ordinary intelligence one key issue of dharma, Nature. When and how did your transformation into the *paishaachic* stage begin?

Everything transforms into its contrary state. This is scientific truth. It is logical and natural that man should transmute into the spiritual state. Eerie evolution! It begins while man still moves in the sphere of the earth, said PishaachaSarwasvam. Hence the fact that radical mutations raged in my body while I was still alive.

Then Pishaacha Sarwasvam went on to elaborating the paishaachic changes that wracked his body.

I found release from the body while still alive. The webbing of the world and relationships were razored. Purling into a phantom, *pretaatma*, is an evolutionary act. Stretched taut to thinning, long ago, the act snapped the thread of my *aatman* from the language of my people and my ambience. Knowledge transformed the earth into cosmos. Everything stopped affecting me even while I wandered on earth in my elemental body – *paanchabhoutika*. And I, too, had stopped affecting anything. A slightness of Being; no specific Gravity. If I left a tea cup in space, it stood, never fell. Levity lightened the body. Why the earth so drastically lost its power of attraction, one can not tell. What modern transformations muted the earth's attraction so absolutely I could not understand. In all, my body lost its bodiness, ceased bodying forth. That is why death did not cause mortal experience. After all, mortality had crawled in and around me since long! With death came release from even the tiny string of gravity that had held me.

Now I can go to the British Museum Library, I can insinuate myself into anything. The other day I went to the White House. I kissed the dearest relations of Master George Bush at the White House during Christmas – India and the Hindu… his pets, a cat and pup.To give the job a neat fininsh, I also kissed his wife – not a squeak out of you, by the way! mind you. I do not need a visa. I could go across the oceans as I pleased. I can travel international without hindrance, as I wished, with a song on my lips – imagine no countries, imagine no hills, imagine no deserts, no rain forests, too; imagine all the governments, no one profiling you…you may say I'm a dreamer, but I'm th'Oly ghost – Leh Non,[12] I believe.

But international flying does not offer me any experience or pleasure. Nothing tangible, nothing tactile. This is the problem with being a pishaacha. Nightmarish perception. Paishaachic experience began while I still lived. Upon death, it became ripe and full. This is a nightmarish look-alike of the free state. That's why I, an airy nothing, am pining for corporeal frame, a body with a local habitation and name.[13] Bawdy with senses, body with a feel for touch. I'll go on, blindly, looking. Touching without tingling; kissing without feeling.

So, you will succeed. Have you before now? Should you fail?

I fail.[14] As there are oceans full of brinish water… not potable, so are there bodies, no bodies at all. No Body seems a good host. No livable structure. Constructed with concrete; cramped, confined, ill-ventillated. No feel, no touch, no senses. O' dull senses, vacuous looks and holdless grasps, O' tuneless airs, bloodless bodies, fleshless bones, what a waste my inquisitor, devastating throng of unthrilling bodies! A vast, vast waste! cried the hapless ghost, Sarwasvam.

Is this, Birsa Munda's, the body you searched for, asked Kanchinaadham.

No this is a body shrunk by colonial education. This is a foreign land. An England. This is a colonial prison. An unshakeable addiction to colonial knowledge has entrapped me in Munda's colonial frame. When I was alive, I lived as a prisoner to colonial knowledge. Now, said Sarwasva Pishaacham, I have turned into a prisoner in the body of Birsa Munda, a colonial prison.

Who forced you into this prison?

A parrot, accustomed to living in a cage, will not accept freedom even if allowed to go. The breadth of the sky renders it breathless. So it will search out the cage and imprison itself. That is exactly my situation. I can not tolerate freedom. Nor can I live as a prisoner. Mine is a curious tragedy, sobbed Sarwasvam, remanded to Munda's body.

At that very time, Sarwasvam's memorial ceremony was being conducted. Intellectuals averred that he was probably the last genius, last critic, the last thinker, because he had broken Telugu's connection with itself. That's why, they asserted, Sarwasvam was the last Telugu man. Then they remained silent in homage to the departed soul, prayed for its peace. Lodged in Munda's body, Sarwasvam wept because he could never find peace.

He roared with paishaachic power, I'll not let your souls rest in peace. An unsatisfied *pretaatma* can not tolerate peace in anyone. It is an accurst being. No one can escape the restlessness it can generate.

4

Sarwasvam's transformation into a pishaacha, restless globe-trotting, incarnation in Birsa Munda's body are undoubtable facts. But there is no currency, no linguicity for some facts in this modern world. Such facts do not come under the purview of modern causality. The language of cause and effect does not offer space for such discussion. But that was the real world in which Kanchinaadham was now cantering around. Thus, while it was a fact that Sarwasvam had turned into a ghost, Kanchinaadham invited trouble for himself by accepting and voicing the fact.

Even Birsa Munda's better-half flew into a rage and berated him. What ghosts! What possession! Science won't accept it. You speak much too much like an idiot. You ignoramus! taunted she.

All his friends concluded that he was dogmatic and orthodox. He was date-expired. What the hell ghosts and ghouls, they said, condemning him for such beliefs in a world which now boasted of computers! In an age when rockets were penetrating deep into the intergalactic spaces of the cosmos, where is the place for ghosts and ghouls? they asked with sarcasm. This is a delusion of the mind, a psychedelic state. Hallucinations. Schizophrenia. Necrotic zeitgeist. Narcosis.

Kanchinaadham did not mind, did not give up. Okay, call me an idiot, brand me a bumpkin; but let me tell you, I have known this right from my childhood, this paishaachic behaviour. Without doubt this is Sarwasvam's ghost, its loud bawl, reverberating through the cosmos.

Kanchinaadham, for the first time in life, proceeded to write an article. Its argument was that one can not understand the human world unless one also grasps the nuances of the world of spirits. Uderstanding the accurst, unsatisfied wanderings of a dead man's soul entailed the knowledge of the ghostly world. Intellectual life is doomed to incompleteness unless one had an analytic knowledge of demonology. The burden of the essay was that the human and the demon were symbiotic, engagingly complementary, almost romantically entailing.

The day after its publication, it was roundly condemned by all. They were unanimous in criticizing it as the worst of the anti-progressive writings of the last one hundred years. They compared Kanchinaadham to computer virus and opined that such a person's existence was worthless.

Some intellectuals were especially vigorous in their response. Ghosts may exist. But talking about them is not a modern way. Modern language does not accommodate ghosts. Ghosts do not submit themselves to modern rationalism. In the event, they advised avuncularly, it was statesmanlike to be calm and silent about ghosts.

Kanchinaadham wrote again – If ghosts are a blind-belief, so is man a blind-belief. It must be a universally acknowledged scientific truth, he said, that magnificent Man himself was evolving into a superhuman spirit, *ubermencht.* This fact was told by an extraordinarily intelligent, brilliant ghost. Such being the truth, maintaining a studied silence about ghosts amounted to maintaining studied silence about Man. He explained, with facile conveniece – *Pishaacha* was an inevitable stage in the evolution of the world.

Meanwhile Thopella Sankaram went the way of all flesh. Hanumantha Rao *aka* Birsa Munda, was left eternally in the possession of ghosts. There was no spiritual nirvana for him.

Kanchinaadham was banished with his very first writing. Each sentence of his was utterly condemnable, it was resolved. Sarvaswam vanished, Kanchinaadham banished. He was exiled from the language of the moderns. Past became *pishaacha* and trailed Kanchinaadham.

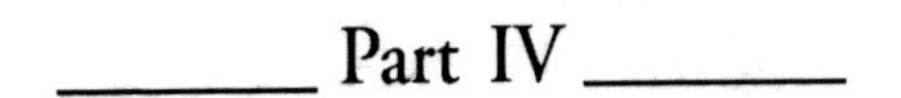

Part IV

Earth is cradle.
Man cannot forever remain in cradle.
– Russian Astronomer

1

Bhoolokam is a painter.

Earth is surpassable. Bholokam's deep desire is to take wing and soar far away from earth.

His constant grief is that everything binds him and pulls him downward.

Bhoolokam is an artist. All his paintings are drawn in circles round the theme of escape – surpassing and escaping. He has painted different kinds of birds, aeroplanes and rockets in a variety of collages. Similarly, he has given shape to strange beings which seem to go past distant stars. His making is a world of wonders.

That man should continue to live on earth, is very tragic, felt Bhoolokam. He thought man was imprisoned in the arms of the earth. He lived, constantly annoyed by bondage.

Everything should be expressible, capable of manifestation. There is nothing that man can not body-forth. What is bodied-forth is exceeded, surpassed. It slips into the scope of human control. Through his expressive ability, man is drawing this world into his control – such was his belief.

Bhoolokam is gifted with great expressive powers. A great artist who could give form to the most complex thought. His words also glow with expressive brilliance. He is quite the contrary of Kanchinaadham. Strangely, divinely ordained perhaps, a friendship developed between the two.

Bhoolokam had recently travelled all through the country. He undertook this journey to peep into the most unlikely caves tucked away in most unknown places. He peered into the depths of those darknesses. He heard them echo calls to calls. He saw many people who still lived in caves. He saw the outlines of ancient man, eyes aggoggle. Saw wondrous paintings in those caves. He encountered the ever so long journey of man, from his first faltering steps to his amazing civilizations, in those recesses of the caves.

The caves appeared like the inner theatre of man. Their secret darknesses shrouded many, many sacred truths. Bhoolokam had heard local people speak of these caves having secret tunnels and pathways to far-away regions and how they had, over the ages, closed. He heard the tale of an emperor who rode secretly through the cave on his horse, Panchakalyaani. Another story went that a king escaped his enemy via the cavernous mouth. He heard many such woven and webbed legends.

Bhoolokam recognized that ancient lines, scripts, drawings, pictograms and paintings, theologies, rise and fall of empires – in essence, the essence of human existence, was all sequestered inside the inner theatres of these caverns, awaiting rediscovery.

Why, he wondered, did man undertake such a long journey within this interiority of the caverns? Is man's journey itself an exploration of this interiority? Is man condemned to eternal introspection ? Did it mean that the unexpressed is the better part of the expressed? Did it imply that there are deep darknesses, unconscious dreams beyond the scope of human creative-vision? Should it be understood that they have the ultimate control of man? Did the ancients believe that truth will be unveiled in the extreme solitude of the cavernous inner theatre?

Several such thoughts raged in Bhoolokam when he was wandering inside those deep caves. Promptly he would call a halt to the resonances strummed within these hollows. Perhaps these hollows were only lateral inversions of these frequent cosmic quests. Real vibrations and true, living, excited sounds inhabit this external world. The inner sonics were only a resonance of this substantial, external reality.

Bhoolokam believed that it was sheer ignorance to imagine that the outer world was only a reflected image of the inner world. Such ignorance was a hindrance to modern man's limitless interest in excavatory archaeology – a relentless digging to bring forth the entrails, to scoop out and eviscerate the coelom of the immanent world into The Manifest.

So he snipped all those contrary thoughts in the bud.

One day a discussion on Buddhist frescoes in caves took place between Kanchinaadham and Bhoolokam.

Bhoolokam observed that Buddha's meditative sculptures convey us, too, into formless worlds. No other historical figure has been delineated as distinctively, delicately and as variously as the Buddha's figure.

Kanchinaadham agreed wholeheartedly. Buddha's innumerable forms come to our minds before the unique Buddhist thought does, he said. The Buddha, continued Kanchinaadham, has spread like woods and meshed into the web of the world, countries and continents as countless figural forms.

Bhoolokam added pensively, that is not all...the Buddha appears lost in that wood's dense form.

Why do you think so? asked Kanchinaadham.

Because, reminded Bhoolokam, Buddha opposed worship of form. He had taught that the bigger the form the greater its needs. Belly bulges barrenly as form fills up.

But, said Kanchinaadham, the Buddha was himself the cause of this formal largesse.

Bhoolokam fell to wondering why that happened. One who had clashed with iconofilia; had taught the importance of free-will through the axiom – *ath thadeepo ath thadhammo* (you are the Light, you are your Guide); why did he get enmeshed in this tradition of name and form, a plurality of figures? Why was he transfigured into the numerous incarnations of legends and translated into the story-tradition of the Jaataka tales ? Why did he get trapped in the tradition of thousand names and thousand forms? Questions flew thick and fast from Bhoolokam.

Everything transforms into its contradiction, said Kanchinaadham, dissolves into its other. True, Buddha forbade the worship of his form. Indeed commanded peremptorily not to preserve his form in any manner. Even this stern command transformed completely into its other.

How? asked Kanchinaadham, and proceeded to narrate a popular legend about the imagination shaping the Buddha.

Buddha had said times without number not to worship him. He had prohibited the making of his shape. He refused to be portrayed in paintings. His disciples heard him in reverent attention. Then they began to consider clever ways of overcoming these directions. The human heart wants to do exactly what it is prohibited to do. It reaches for the forbidden. This is a critical aspect of human psychology. Meaning, the psyche ineluctably strives into its other. Exactly this happened.

One staunch faithful got a clever idea. He made fuzzy line-drawing basing it on the Buddha's shadow. I told you not to draw my picture, said an angry, livid, Tathaagata.

I drew your shadow, Shaakyamuni! Not your form! said the disciple, wittily. The disciple had thus created a breach in the discipline, a narrow crevice which other idle imaginations could widen for formal purposes.

Eventually a path had been found for a pluri-formal Buddhist iconography. Even the Buddha could not halt this evolution, the march towards manifestations. Thus a staunch opponent of form, the Buddha himself became an idol and made way for idol-worship, concluded Kanchinaadham.

You are, said Bhoolokam, doubting language itself. Saying, ayes and noes constantly glide into each other, always slipping into their contrary states. Then language will always fail. The weave of words turns into a dense wood of unmeaning sounds, leading to psychic delusions and a push into endless darkness. Language, man's most significant creative invention, will enter into its own death in a suicidal move, said an anguished Bhoolokam.

If your logic is admitted, language gets trapped between dualities, *dwandwa*. Dualism entails a constant transformational movement, yo-yo like. Stances change infinitely, making consistency impossible. A definite, determinate, clear expression becomes impossible. So language stops reflecting Reality. Indeed, no scope itself exists for Reality. Expression curls itself up into a black cat in a an unlit chamber, said Bhoolokam expressing his grief at this turn of thought.

Kanchinaadham reinforced the idea – No one can escape this constant mutual morphing of the contraries. It is ceaseless. Heat and cold, joy and sorrow are not really different from each other. That is why nil becomes full, nothing becomes something, and rejection translates into acceptance. A prohibition of idol-worship compels itself into its contrary, a rising idolatry. That is what happened to Christianity. Jesus was deeply opposed to formal worship, had idols rejected. But with the phenomenal progress of Christian art, the opposition lost much intensity. Iconoclasm transformed itself into worship of form.

Within the Bharatakhanda itself, there is much indifference towards the material world; indeed a great detachment. Strong is he who is disinterested, it is said ... *udaasiinoo mahaabalah*. That is why there are no clear forms of gods. Acharyas such as Shankara, and philosophers, also have no specific form. There is no one who can authoritatively claim and carry popular conviction that such is the sole representable form. No one has drawn an indisputably clear and authentic form of gods and seers. There may at the most be hazy signs.

Actually, there is no idol-worship in the *Vaidic karmakaanda*, scriptural ritual. In the sacrificial rituals of the Vaidic kind, there is no deistic idolism, only a purifying rite of the element Fire, *Agni*. In the *vaidica samskara*, rites of passage such as the *upanayana*, *vivaaha* and *shraaddha* – initiation, marriage and obsequies – there is no idol-worship, no figure, only figurality. Again, in the *vaidica dharma*, there is no identifiable prophet.

Interestingly, idol-worship gained momentum and strength only after the advent of Buddhism. Bouddha, which was opposed to idol-worship, itself gave a strong impetus to the expansive spread of idol-worship. Being opposed to form, Bouddha nonetheless got embroiled in an infinitely iconic Buddhist formalism. Bouddha had asserted that the form of the Buddha had no significance, no primacy whatsoever. The Buddha had taught as much. Yet, preservation of the Buddha's bones and hair as relics for worship formed into a Buddhist tradition. Jaataka tales sprang around him. In these tales the Buddha assumes many lives and incarnations for the betterment of the world. In these stories he had turned into an incarnation of God. I'll take body in every Age, *Sambhavaami Yuge Yuge*, he said. Eventually the concept of Vishnu's avatars emerged, inspired by *Bouddha*. What's more, the Buddha who inspired the Dashaavataara of Vishnu, himself became one of the avatars. The cause became the effect. The beginning curls into the end. This is how everything transforms into its contradiction. Dissolves into its other.

Kanchinaadham paused, then resumed. He returned to his favourite turf, Sanaatana Dharma.

Nonchalance is the hallmark of Sanaanatana. Hence the lack of clear form for its gods and seers, despite the singular influence of Bouddha and its art. There are no specific legends, no authentic shapes. All is Signification. All Abstraction. Dispassion is the reason for this state, Kanchinaadham explained.

Immigrant Christians shook this insouciance. A fundamental change occurred. Ravi Varma is a prime example of this change.

Ravi Varma drew inspiration from Christian art. His inspiration gave form to all gods. He gave inhabitable, authentic form to all Pauraanic figures and to incarnations. He gave shapes to seers such as Shankara. He stuck European faces to all these folk. Faces of the Caucasian race. He created forms in the true style of immigrant Christian art; a thorough imitation, he did, of faces and forms already in full view. That is how they found popular acceptance.

Macaulay's Christian educational policies colonialized the Indians. Ravi Varma's Judeo-Christian depictions appeared authentic to their colonized sensibilities. This is the origin of Hindu art. Hindu art emerged from the very Christianity which opposed idol-worship. Accepted Hindu forms rose from the perfect iconoclastic principles of an imperialistic Christian tradition, said Kanchinaadham.

Bhoolokam opened up in reply.

Communists are the only true iconoclasts, he said. Communists totally oppose sycophant devotion. Only the Master's word, only the principle, only the practice is important to communism; not formal worship, not a devotion to the individual. Indeed sycophancy is anathema to communism, said Bhoolokam. They practise what they profess – the very firstlings[15] of their thought are the firstlings of their action. Hence there is no contradiction in their wor(l)d. Bhoolokam tried to hold the communists up as an example to contradict Kanchinaadham's theory.

No one has invited more idolatry than the great communist teachers, said Kanchinaadham. They have outdone the Bouddhas and the Christians in this respect.

The Bouddhas have made figures of the Buddha and worshipped those figures. They turned his bones and hair into relics and worshipped those relics. Christians composed paintings of Christ, captured him in colours and sang carols to him. Truly, Bouddhas and Christians behaved contrary to the teaching of their prophets.

But communists went much farther in their idolatry. They preserved the bodies of great communist masters in chemicals and put them on exhibition. They chose to preserve those masters as long as the sun and the moon lasted. They resolved to worship them forever.

That's how Communists turned into greater idol-worshippers than all religious ideologues. They aspired to transforming all the people of the world into their state. Mao's formulation that everything transforms itself into its contrary, applies chiefly to Marxists themselves – said Kanchinaadham.

Theism transforms into atheism. Cause transforms into conviction; reason turns into belief. Man's imagination, his ability to engage in fancy, is the origin of reason as well as faith. Science attempts to understand faith through mathematical equations. Mathematics steals silently into formless worlds. Mathematics is the highest form of human imagination. Hence rationality is merely imagination, a fantastic belief. All belief is born of imagination. That is why that which is imagined to be rational turns into faith. Thus ideologies such as apparently rational communism ossify into religious faiths. Because ... imagination, being *swayambhu, sui generis*, is the genesis of both rationality and faith. Everything is born of the human mind which is illuminated by imagination. In this vast space of the mind everything undergoes change, and results in its contradiction. This is a ceaseless process.

There are many instances illustrating this principle. These examples are available in the practices of communism itself. Capitalist barons emerged from the band of communists who strongly opposed private property. From socialists who opposed sheer generation of wealth came great avatars of Fortune Five-Hundred. Those who claimed strong devotion to the cause of tribals and Harijans unleashed merciless massacre on them, not sparing even children. This, said Kanchinaadham, with the finality of breaking the clay-pot at a cremation, is the form of the world, a union of contraries.

He proceeded to cite contemporary Hindu history. Those who indulge in sloganeering entailing violence, to save the Sanaatana Dharma – those very proponents of Hindutva are making the graveyard ready for the *Samadhi* of the Sanaatana Dharma. Be it known that, that which is zealously guarded, is destroyed and dead, said Kanchinaadham.

In support of this proposition that All transforms into its contrary, he further cited a Pauraanic fable. There was a great aasuric nobleman of the name Hiranyakashipa. He conquered the whole world; then he went into a fierce state of *tapas,* meditation. Brahma appeared before him and offered him a boon. What did Hiranyakashipa seek? A very curious boon! That there be no death for him by either man or beast; at daytime or at night. In sum a cleverly stated immortality. He got the boon; but did not escape death. Interestingly, said Kanchinaadham, mortality is embedded in immortality. It lurks like a thorn among flowers. So, death confronted Hiranyakashipa in an unimaginable form. It was neither day nor night – twilight; neither man nor beast – Narasimha man-lion. Narasimha killed Hiranyakashipa in the twilight hour. One who hoped to deny death, was subjected to the crullest death imaginable. Intense desire for immortality, led to mortality. Everything gets transformed into its other.

In effect, sheer indifference towards something is the equivalent of confronting it – *udasiino mahaabalah*; he who is stoic is the most powerful one in this world, said Kanchinaadham as a final drum-roll at a concert.

2

Indifference leads to inertia. It ends in inaction, said Bhoolokam. Inaction is contrary to the creative impulse; it opposes contructivity. Lack of constructivity among Brahmins is the direct fall-out of their theorizing of detachment. There is no constructivity anywhere in their literature or in their logic, he said. That's why India has no history, no religion...

Kanchinaadham replied – *saguna* and *nirguna* converge at the same point. Form and formlessness become one. Shivalinga is form, but it is also formless. Shivalinga has neither human nor animal form. Even a formless, assymmetrical rock is worshipped as God. It has form if you say so; has no form if you say no. It is Nature's nature to be formless, without a clear, symmetric form. Symmetry and arrangement relate to human perception; they do not exist in the outer world. Perception is Creation. *Drishti is Srishti.*

Man sees this world in some particular way. Experiences it in one way through his senses. Tries to measure it with his mind. All his measures are empirical and limited. They are subject to the limitations of the body, senses and intelligence. His measures are limited by his own creations – culture and civilization, and the language that signifies them. They are not esoteric, not final judgments, said Kanchinaadham.

My word is that man's theories and his scriptural professions are not absolute – they originate in man's mind and incinerate there itself. There is, said Kanchinaadham, no substantive Truth anywhere in this world.

Bhoolokam came back at him – Man does not just perceive, and comment on, this world. He changes it. He creates a new world. He experiences birth-pangs. He derives joy from it. Bhoolokam cited the examples of scientists and their inventions. He lauded the enterprise of man who conquered time and distance.

What's this new creation, asked Kanchinaadham, sarcastically. Whose birth-pangs? Whose joy? Columbus set foot on the American continent. He made it known to the white masters. What did they do? They cleansed the place of the natives through extreme violence. They eradicated the native's languages. They superimposed their culture-civilization. Whose victory was this? Whose loss?

Modern man's creative-play wove one more illusion. We can never see 'the truth' through that complex weave. Reality has turned into the greatest delusion. Modern creativity is nothing but a web of illusions, said Kanchinaadham. A magic that dims our vision.

3

Bhoolokam had not given up. Modernity, he asserted, tears through all illusion. It rips through all mysteries and reveals the reality. Now there are no more secrets; there is no mysterious mantle, no magic, said Bhoolokam, dismissing Kanchinaadham's views. The scope for creativity and expression has grown more than ever. An expansive world of imagination has come into existence. Modernity has opened the doorways of imagination; will continue to do so. Just as it appears in the material world, it also manifests in amazing artistic work.

Bhoolokam displayed all his paintings as an example of the great talent of the new world. They were amazing paintings. It was true that extraordinary imaginative powers shimmered through them. His art appeared as if thought had assumed colours, soared on wings. It felt, possibly, like the first ever flight in the first ever airplane.

Kanchinaadham's perception, however, was different. He was full of admiration towards Bhoolokam's paintings. Yet, at the same time, that imagination, that creativity, terrified him. He wondered whether Bhoolakam had not become a prisoner of his imaginary world. Bird songs are very sweet. Where does it lead the birds? Into the cage. Imagination imprisons man.

Man is greatly disturbed when the birds cackle... when that imaginary world shows cracks. This is the recurrent story from time before life's memory. Man created many imaginary heavens – utopias. He embraced much violence to sustain them. Still, they exploded, and left man thwarted and disappointed. This has been a timeless process.

Bhoolokam strongly believes that imagination will grow wings and free us from earth's gravity. Kanchinaadham views imagination as an unassailable prison. They are distinct affirmations.

Many women loved Bhoolokam. His words are magnetic. He is highly creative and imaginative – makes worlds not just with a paint brush, but with the romance of words, too. His wit mesmerizes the best of them. In consequence, a married woman developed such closeness, was so enchained to him, that she plunged into a canal and committed suicide – she could not accept separation from him. It was impossible to hold, to own a man who was always in flight on the wings of incontinence.

Bhoolokam's fantastic ability, therefore, is terrific and death-dealing. After all, creation and curtailment, deed and death are mutually entailing!

Bhoolokam is like a singing bird that has sweet expressive power.

Kanchinaadham is a crow that caws.

No one cages a crow. So it lives on, safely, peacefully. Its voice is wretched, its looks loathsome. It lacks expression. Kanchinaadham lacks expression. For Kanchinaadham, this lack has turned into luck. There is a lack of purpose in his very existence. Vacancy and waste – inform his existence. No one binds him; he binds none. That's why, lady love, Saroja, left so easily.

In modern times everyone seeks the novel.

Bhoolokam's desire for novelty shows, artist that he is. Countless wealthy men eagerly wish to decorate their newly designed mansions with his paintings. They are more attracted by his paintings than the latest brands of cars. They willingly spend more money on his paintings than on the latest cars in market. They deem it a symbol of status to buy his paintings. There are many wealthy men who prefer gifting Bhoolokam's latest paintings to their mistresses, than buying them a diamond necklace.

There is no such desire in Kanchinaadham. There is a vacuum in place of desire.

4

Nothing new ever comes into the world, said Kanchinaadham. Great expansion collapses into great contraction. The world is so curved. One comes back to an original point. Nothing... nothing new happens, thundered Kanchinaadham. There is no new creation, he exploded, his word as final as the shattered funeral pot.

That's alright, said Bhoolokam. But is it true that Sarvaswam has become a fiend and now haunts Birsa Munda?

Yes, that's true, said Kanchinaadham.

They are different poles, different views. One is a communist, the other an ultra-modernist. Their union is an astonishing happening. Something new must have come out of such a union, asserted Bhoolokam.

That's just delusion. Your artistic mind makes you think so. You achieve a sense of novelty by making a hodge-podge of contrary, unrelated things. You call it creativity. You are trying to apply the same principle here. Nothing new ever emerges from mere experimentation, said Kanchinaadham.

He announced again, there is really nothing that is new.

Bhoolkam joined issue – that's wrong. Science has unveiled much that was never accessible before.

No, said Kanchinaadham. Nothing new. Science is governed by tradition, sanaatana. The kaarmic principle underlies the scientific view that the universe turns on certain pre-determined laws. Karma is cyclicality. Born again... dead again. No scope for the new.

Bhoolokam disagreed. This world is the symbol of eternal newness. This universe came to exist through a huge explosion, the Big Bang. A manifest world with name and form came to be. A new, four-dimensional world came into existence then. This is the source of creation. A similar explosion occurs in a poet and an artist. That leads to creation.

Kanchinaadham denied that the world was ever created. Creation defies logic. Logic demands causation. The universe is without beginning, without end. Where is the scope for ideas of new and old in a world that has no beginning, no end? There is no ground for imagining anything new. Creation is an illusory cycle. Just that.

It is incorrect to assume a beginning for the world. Such an assumption is only a Christian belief. That belief has gained currency, is indeed masquerading as science.

If there is a beginning for the universe, the possibility of sequence and order emerges. Imagining a Creator becomes possible. Calling that creator God, becomes easy. Suggesting that that God created an order and a logicality becomes possible. All of this can happen only if it can be asserted that creation began on one day; that there was a beginning. If a beginning could be asserted, an end becomes a logical conclusion. If Creation is true then cataclysm is true, too. This world is no more than a series of events. If one could discover the beginning and the end of this world, one could assign a logical sequence and a history to it. On the other hand, if it were impossible to propose a beginning, what would happen to logic, and what would history mean?

A God as Creator, an evolutionary logic, and an apocalypse are Christian beliefs. A modern world-view has sprung from these beliefs. Such a view is the genesis of a 'systematic' history. History is the result of a causal view. That is why the Catholic Church supported the Big Bang theory – that there was a mega explosion and the ever expanding world emerged from ...

But creation has no beginning, no end ...it is *anaadi, anantha.* Expression comes from the unexpressed. The expressed dissolves into the unexpressed. The substantial world comes from the micronic. The micronic is also the universal solvent. This is an endless, infinite dynamics of re-solvent substance. Cause contains effect in a reflexive state. Tree is planted in seed, as seed grows on tree. Nothing new comes. In fact, nothing comes. That's why contraries become integral. Everything transforms into its other. Dissolves into its other. Always. And Resolves again. Always.

All of the Universe

Is the Shrine of m' Lord

Street-front, back yard, how matter Sister![16]

The Rear... A Nightmare

I eased myself into bed, happy that Grahaantaravaasi was completed. I went into a deep slumber in no time. A dream caught me napping.

Friend Narahari and I were strolling along the canal banks. Narahari said, the earth is about to end.

I skidded into a surprise, then recovered quickly. Probably you speak about a few crore years.

No. No... the earth is ending in just a little time. Narahari let his words explode, terrifyingly. The globe will get destroyed; its surface will blow and swell; it will expand and spread beyond the atmosphere, into space. The sky which creates the atmosphere, time, and space between objects – the sky itself will vanish. It will not be possible to call that dead surface by the name earth. That is ghoulish matter. Its expansion is demonic. The earth will definitely end, asserted Narahari.

I rose, startled. Anxiety stopped me from sleeping again. Sleep was banished. Nightmare reigned. I spun into the cosmos. Beyond its pale. Where Kanchinaadham was!

May be.

When Narahari's earth explodes, Kanchinaadham, the intergalactic will not mourn. Because the nightmare has always been. And with tiny beruffled wings drawn in, KK sits brooding, waiting for the contrary turn he may or not have missed. Which may or may not have happened.

The Earth-bound and the Apocalyptic – An Afterword

When I woke Sarma one midnight via the telephone trunkline, my intention was to tell him how thrilled I was to read the first page of Grahaantaravaasi. That was in 2006.

Soon I was speaking away in my usual stop-start style about how happy I will be if he let me translate the work.

He agreed!

We were strangers a minute ago, and had been transformed into friends (not acquaintances) in the true spirit of Grahaantaravaasi.

True to that spirit, we will become strangers some day.

But I think both of us have the strength of the stoics – udaasiino mahaabala.

We will accept the transformation as easily as we spoke that night 3 years ago.

What's it about Rani Sarma and Grahaantaravaasi that binds us ?

We are probably the contraries which keep mutating into each other. He is Telugu, authentic. I am the English quotation. He is swadeshi. I am hybrid.(not yet courageous enough to call myself a mimic)

Rajeshwara Rao, my longtime friend, who gifted me Sarma's book and caused us to meet, is like Kanchinaadham. Out there, where only he can roam, whiskey and cigarette in hand, convinced about the triviality of what most of us find very serious business. Cheers, friend. All the questions, all the convictions, all the characteristics of Kanchinaadham parading live, yet in a vacuum only Rajeshwara can inhabit.

Kanchinaadham is the Naatha, LordGod, of Kanchi – a symbol of all the contraries our world may experience. He is the world. He is the Revealed Truth, the ultimate vision, an epiphany we may have in its most wondrous, and its most terrifying form.

Bhoolokam represents our rootedness to earth, the boring, galling globe.

This is a book that all the earth-bound may read to experience the great escape of Kanchinaadham. Kanchinaadham is the apocalyptic in its many-splendoured hues. He shows us how we are eternal.The apocalypse is in the revelation, not in the disastrous ending we are taught to fear.

Knowing Bhoolokam is to fear.

Knowing Kanchinaadham is to find release from fear.

The Idiom

Friends who were troubled by my 'approach' to the work deserve an explanation from me; this might also help other similarly 'troubled' readers. My 'adaptation', its technique (or lack of it), is a matter of significance to me, and perhaps these friends (among the readers I hope this book will reach), will see the 'logic', even if they can not agree with it.

The first thing I wish to state here is that I did not 'translate' Rani Sivasankara Sarma's work *Grahaantaravaasi*; I adapted it into English. I believe that translation in toto is impossible – not because of all the usual reasons cited such as cultural, grammatical, semantic differences between the languages, which are indeed perfectly genuine reasons; but because I believe that translation is only one of the tools in the process of re-rendering a work in another language. This re-rendering, is what I have chosen to term 'adaptation' which is a much more inclusive term than the limiting term 'translation'. The relationship of equivalences which translation imposes on the processes of re-rendering, narrows down the text's prospect of living in another language with minimal loss of the original richness of the author's original text. Mathematical precision is impossible because the ecology of each language is at least subtly different if not boldly extreme. The rain-punctuated English summer and the baking heat of an Indian summer can hardly provide translators an adequate lexis of smooth equivalences. Indeed, the heat and dust of Rajasthan and the sultriness and humidity of coastal Andhra Pradesh and TamilNadu are hardly interchangeable in experience and language. English education and primary school geography classes will not change 'shadrithu' into four seasons.

The 'twilight' of England and the fortnight of a polar daylight will not describe the 'asurasandhya' of India's Sanskritic languages which at once connote the physical phenomenon and the cultural associations with 'sura'(divine) and 'asura'(demonic), an entire angelology /demonology which the west can not easily access. The transition from light to darkness is a transition from the 'time' of the heavenly/divine, to the time of the netherworld/ demonic and thereby hangs an entire cultural and ethical story.

That cultural transformation of twilight and night is possible (perhaps ?) only in a phrase such as 'demonic-dusk', (*asura* + *sandhya*); 'twilight' is too light an expression to carry the load of the Telugu adjectival with its origin in Sanskrit.

The second point I wish to elaborate is the technical difference in the syntax of Telugu and English. It is simplistic to state the obvious that the structures are different. What the dubhashi must look at is the implications and ambiguities this difference engenders.

I rendered one sentence in Telugu into an 'English' structure as:

> *"The one who freed Subbamma from epilepsy was Hymavathi, Sambayya Deekshitulu's disciple's wife!"*

A proper Anglo-American sentence would perhaps be

> *Sambayya Deekshitulu's disciple's wife, Hymavathi, was the one who freed Subbamma from epilepsy.*

Closer still would be:

> *Hymavathi, the wife of Sambayya Deekshitulu's disciple, was the one who freed Subbamma from epilepsy.*

Let us look at the grammatical segments of this sentence:

a.	Hymavathi,	*Subject*
b.	The wife of Sambayya Deekshitulu's disciple,	*Relative Clause* (functioning as noun clause)
c.	was	*Verb*
d.	the one who freed Subbamma from epilepsy.	*Subject complement*

However one can see from the Telugu structure that *b. is a description, a qualifier, hence its function is adjectival, not nominal.*

The segment *d.* also is a description, a qualifier, serving adjectivally, not merely as an *subject complement* telling us what Hymavathi *achieved* but that Hymavathi may be described as

Subbamma's apothecary/counselor. Hymavathi is yet again to be described as 'disciple's wife' and Saambayya Deekshitulu's disciple's wife. There are four (4) descriptive/adjectival segments here, all of them *relative* segments, each one a subject complement relative to the Subject Hymavathi, but should technically be Noun phrases. There is an inference to be drawn here – that in Telugu it is possible to load a sentence with adjective after adjective in the manner of Sanskrit, which English rules out, for the sake of precision or economy or both. Adaptation will be more effective if there is an attempt to retain the Telugu structures as long as they do no harm to the objective of an English rendering. *Real damage* would be a pucca English rendering, in which case one might as well have rewritten the work with fidelity to English syntax.

Given the fact that Sarma's work is rather a contestation of English, indeed, western values as such, imagine the disservice to his work that would ensue if it were rendered into pucca English with a stiff lip and a pencil moustache!

So, I have tried to practice my dictum that the text must be sufficiently different in its use of English to indicate that it emerges from another culture, another language. I have taken some liberties with the language as well as the original text to keep my English adaptation enjoyable. Trying to practice my 'Fruit of the Mango tree' method – (See note 17 for excerpts) – Successfully? I must say, I tried earnestly. Perhaps someone else will be able to practice it better with some other text.

I wish other practitioners much success.

And I think this book can do with some success as well.

G.K.Subbarayudu

Some Notes

1. "As destiny assigned, so duly suffered" (*Ea paatu vidhincheno vidhi adi avasya praapthamaou*), from the ever popular stage play – the story of *Satya Harishchandra.*
2. "King become commoner, attender turn emperor, in tune with the diktat of eternal time" (*raaje kinkarudavu kinkarudavu raju, kaalaanukuulambunan*), cf. Note 1.
3. "Know this is dream/ nor know this is real / know this is life/ yes, know this is life" (*kala yidanee nijamidanee, teliyadulee, bathukinthenulee, inthenulee*). From the Telugu film *Devadas* based on the acclaimed Bengali novel, *Devdas* (1917), of Sharat Chandra Chattopadhyay. Very popular song sung by Ghantasala.
4. "World is illusion, life is illusion, this, O man, is the simple essence of the Vedas" (*jagamae maya, batthukee maya, vedaalaloo saaraminthenayaa*). From the Telugu film *Devadas* (cf. Note 3) One more popular song, again sung by Ghantasala.
5. Silence is manifest commentary on the nature of the Divine Ultimate (*mouna vyaakhyaa prakatitha parabrahma thathvam*); Adi Shankaracharya...
6. '*nor swoon'd nor utter'd cry*':*Tennyson's well-known poem* "Home They Brought Her Warrior Dead..." (From *The Princess,* Christmas 1847) – Home they brought her warrier dead;/ She nor swoon'd nor utter'd cry. /All her maidens, watching, said, / 'She must weep or she will die.'
7. Sanskrit: *kim satyam, kimasatyaha* – What is true, what is false?
8. *"My seated heart knocks at my ribs, against the use of nature."* Shakespeare. *Macbeth.*, Act I Scene 3.
9. "What bloody man is that? he can *report,* /..., of the revolt /*The newest state."* Shakespeare. *Macbeth.*, Act I Scene 2.
10. *Leaf among tender leaves/ blossom among balmy bowers/ downy soft sepal may I snugly conceal, infuse myself softly in this, thy forest?:* 'Aakulo aakunai, poovulo poovunai' by Devulapalli Venkata Krishna Sastri, a major Telugu poet of a romantic movement along-side Rayaprolu Subba Rao in the 1930s.

11. "Hie thee hither,/That I may pour my spirits in thine ear/ And *chastise with the valor of my tongue*/All that impedes thee from the golden round." Shakespeare. *Macbeth.*, Act I, Scene 5.
12. John Lennon's song *Imagine* (1971), modified suitably; the author, Sarma, uses the Modern Telugu poet Sri Sri's lines from the famous poem "Mahaa Prasthaanam": *Nadi nadaalu / aDavulu KonDalu/ eDaarulaa manakaDDamki?*/padanDi munduku!/ padanDi trosuku!/ Podaam, podaam pai paiki!"(Rivers n' riv'lets/thickets n' mountains/deserts... Are these Impediments?/March on ahead / shove and stampede/ Another world is calling us.) first published in *Mahaa Prasthaanam* (*circa* 1950).
13. "And as imagination bodies forth / The forms of things unknown, the poet's pen/ Turns them to shapes and gives to *airy nothing / A local habitation and a name.*" "Shakespeare. *A Midsummer Night's Dream* Act V, Scene 1.
14. "Macbeth: If we *should fail*? / Lady Macbeth: *We fail*?/ But screw your courage to the sticking-place, /And we'll not fail." Shakespeare. *Macbeth.*, Act I, Scene 7.
15. "From this moment/The *very firstlings* of my heart shall be/ *The firstlings of my hand.*"Shakespeare. *Macbeth.*, Act IV, Scene 1.
16. Devulapalli Krishna Sastri (cf. Note 10), whose *Bhaava kavitvam* is a major landmark in early twentieth century Telugu poetry. *Viswamantaa praanavibhuni mandiramaina/veedhi, vaakili, yedi chellelaa." (Amrutha Veena;* Orient Longman, Hyderabad, 1992, Song 96, p.121)
17. G.K.Subbarayudu, "Re-viewing Fruit of the Mango Tree: From Linguistic Translation to Cultural Adaptation":

    Instead of translation, would it be more useful to think and practice adaptation? Would that provide a more suitable platform from which to practice the rendering of texts from one language into others? Would that be a linguistic act or a cultural performance which would accept as axiomatic cultural translatability through cognition, than linguistic intranslatability owing to perceptual difference?...

    I propose ... that *close adaptation* is a good alternative to transaltional paralysis through theoretical and agendaic moves. Close adaptation *uses* ranslation as one of its tools.... It facilitates the forging of a suitable idiom and enables retelling through several kinds of transcendence. In Act II Scene 1 of *Kanyasulkam*, Gurazada gets Girisam and Venkatesam to 'converse' in English for the benefit of Venkatesam's doting, illiterate mother Venkamma. The farce enacted there is a betrayal of the first order on a trusting mother.

But Gurazada immortalizes Milton's already deathless utterance by a clever act of cultural substitution amounting to a sledgehammer stroke in the course of that conversation: 'Of Man's first disobedience and the fruit of that mango tree, sing Venkatesa, my very good boy' (EMESCO, 1997, P 43; emphasis added) The satirical punch of mango substituting for 'forbidden' from *Paradise Lost,* Bk. I in the farcical allusion is only one dramatic aspect of postcolonial subversion – had the colonial rulers held him answerable to questions of religious and literary blasphemy, Gurazada could comfortably have got out of a spot of bother by pleading 'ignorance' of the great literary tradition, or perhaps even an innocent slip.

For me, Gurazada's 'fruit of that mango tree' is a cultural move that could show the way forward for a viable, creative adaptation. Such adaptation might, in turn, engender a culturally more purposeful critical review than the eulogy of the 'original' text which passes for translation-review today. 'Fruit of that mango tree' comes much closer to the Telugu culture, indeed most Indian cultures, than 'fruit of that forbidden tree' which negates the desirability of any fruit-bearing tree. This cultural desirability transcends linguistic intranslatability and moves towards cultural adaptation.The Late C.Vijayasree and T.Vijaykumar (*Kanyasulkam,* The Book Review Literary Trust, Delhi. 2002.), for instance, manage 'broomance', for *cheepurukatta* (broom) *sarasam* (romantic playfulness). Where plausible equivalents – standard, idiomatic, dialectal, colloquial, culturally accessible, technical, etc., – constitute the domain of the inaccessible, adaptation enables the bilingual project while 'translation' can only impede it (this is best illustrated by the painstaking efforts of state-sponsored language academies, and the ludicrous results of their efforts). The mango-tree is, for me, as much a symbol of cultural adaptation and subaltern rejection/revolt, as an invitation to the reviewer-critic to delve into the complex process unfettered by rigid, deterministic presumptions (and to see that the *apple – mango* example...[is]... analogous... [to the substitution of Sri Sri's verse with Lennon's song])…. The immense flexibility offered to the reviewer-critic is productive of mature study rather than childish tilting-at-windmills which is in practice now. In turn, such review will encourage more multi-lingual literary effort. The fruit of the mango is irresistibly sweet and is an assurance against the 'forbidden' and exclusionist... [principles as in many a reviewer-critic's practice].

— from *Translation Today* Vol.5, No.s 1 & 2,
CIIL, Mysore, 2008.